Praise for DmitryVachedin

"Dmitry Vachedin, an [illegible] author, defines his *Sno*[illegible] 'love among people a[illegible] Russia inside out to disco[illegible]anness he can find, and then does [illegible] to Germany to reveal its Russianness." – *ExLibris*

"This talented émigré author writes vividly about Russians in Germany and Germans in Russia, about love connecting people from different worlds, and how individual human destinies are affected by global social and economic problems." – *Megalit*

"His brilliant prose, obviously influenced by the ideas of Bernard Werber, reads as poetry, not that it is rhymed or metered, but for its metaphorical language and reliance on poetic devices." – *Znamya*

"These stories are overflowing with love, an ocean of overwhelming love, and can be compared with the sensual prose of Anna Gawalda. Vachedin conveys this sensation so vividly that you begin to envy the characters as well feel for them." – *Literary Russia*

"The story of the current events in the novel is intertwined with scenes from the past, family histories, and the history of the 'Snow Germans' as a unique phenomenon in its own right."

– *ZINZIVER literary magazine*

Glas New Russian Writing

contemporary Russian literature

in English translation

Volume 57

This is the seventh volume
in the Glas sub-series
devoted to young Russian
authors, winners and
finalists of the Debut
Prize sponsored by the
Pokolenie Foundation for
humanitarian projects.
Glas acknowledges their
generous support in
publishing this book.

Dmitry Vachedin

SNOW GERMANS

Translated by Arch Tait

GLAS PUBLISHERS
tel./fax: +7(495)441-9157
perova@glas.msk.su
www.glas.msk.su

DISTRIBUTION

In North America
Consortium Book Sales and Distribution
tel: 800-283-3572; fax: 800-351-5073
orderentry@perseusbooks.com
www.cbsd.com

In the UK
CENTRAL BOOKS
orders@centralbooks.com
www.centralbooks.com
Direct orders: INPRESS
Tel: 0191 229 9555
customerservices@inpressbooks.co.uk
www.inpressbooks.co.uk

Within Russia
Jupiter-Impex
www.jupiterbooks.ru

Editors: Natasha Perova & Joanne Turnbull
Cover design by Igor Satanovsky
Camera-ready copy: Tatiana Shaposhnikova

paper book ISBN 978-5-7172-0097-4
ebook ISBN 978-5-7172-0100-1

Contents

SNOW GERMANS is a metaphysical novel about the Volga Germans living in Russia, and their cultural and psychological problems in an alien society against the background of Russo-German relations from Peter the Great to the present. Germans were encouraged to settle in the Russian countryside from the 16th century. Over the ages they tried to preserve their national identity and traditions, but in the 20th century, marked with two great wars which made them highly unpopular, they started repatriating only to find themselves foreigners in their cherished homeland.

The theme of emigration is abundantly relevant today. The emotions and experiences described in *Snow Germans* should be close to many people in the West.

Says the author: "The characters exist in the cross-cultural space between Russia and Germany, a space populated by about three million Russian-speaking Germans, who will soon disappear and probably no longer be around in 50 years. My aim was to depict this disappearing world."

The novel consists of monologues by three protagonists – repatriated Russian Germans – whose lives become entangled at a certain point in the country of law and order, where they suddenly realize that they feel more Russian than German. They find themselves culturally different from their neighbors and often fail to integrate into local communities. On the other hand, they have never felt quite at home in Russia.

Says the translator: "These three young former Volga Germans are uniquely placed to compare the strengths and weaknesses of the Russian and German temperaments, and don't by any means come down unambiguously in favour of orderly Europe. The language is imaginative and the novel a delight to read. A highly topical exploration of the relationships between young people trapped between Europe's poles of Germany and Russia."

DMITRY VACHEDIN was born in 1982 in St Petersburg and moved to Germany with his parents in 1999. He graduated from Johannes Gutenberg University in Mainz with a degree in Political Science and Slavic Studies. Currently he lives in Bonn and works as a journalist for Deutsche Welle.

At the age of 25 he won the Debut Prize for his short stories. In 2010 his novel *Snow Germans* was nominated for the Russian Prize, and in 2012 he became the winner of the Russian Prize for his short stories.

Critics find his writing reminiscent of Nabokov on the one hand and Thomas Mann on the other.

SNOW GERMANS

a novel

VALERIA

"What are you doing?"

Oh, it's like that, is it? Well sucks to you! Sucks to the whole street, to this whole sad city that, the moment I climbed on to this window sill, collapsed quivering at my feet. Not even that: it threw a fit while I trampled on it. This is a city that looks like someone chucked it down off its hill and broke it in three. To my right, the bridge over the railroad; to my left, the main road winding round behind like a fox's tail; and straight in front, on the far side of the air current flowing above the street, apartment blocks that are watching me. That must be a music school, because through the windows I can see violin bows frozen in mid-air, a singer motionless, gaping. Yoo-hoo, sausage makers! I prod the height in front of me with my toe, like provoking a sleeping dog. Am I scaring you yet? Come on, I know you are having dirty little thoughts about my body. Who says no to a Russian girl? You only built this town to get me here, half of it yellow stone and the other half glass because you know we like shiny things, right? Your little trap. Your snare. Because I am for real and you, sad sausage makers, are fake.

"Come down from that window! Get down, do you hear me?"

Shan't! Why spoil the fun for the passersby? I've just invented a new domestic service, nude window cleaning. It's only the cut-price help from Eastern Europe trying to make ends meet. No, don't come any closer or I might forget how high it is up here. Or perhaps not even height is for real in Germany. Perhaps it's just so much playacting and the houses are lying horizontally like on a trick film set. You never look up, so how would you know? Perhaps this window is just as artificial as those fenced-off summits of your sad hills with that sad, spotless bench which is always conveniently nearby. In the city where I was born there isn't a high-rise someone hasn't jumped off. The City of Flying Russians, we call it. People there know all about real height, and how alluring it is. Do you? Like hell you do. Even I was beginning to forget.

"Valeria, are you insane? Put your clothes on at once! Let's talk this through."

Only if you speak Russian. You don't know Russian? Too bad. Damn, it's cold up here. I'm only wearing the clanging of the trams. One's just gone by. It's up on the bridge over the rail tracks now, where the station is, the piston, the pumping heart of the city. Well, sausage makers, I am the nerve the arsenic paralyzes. I'm going to come down from the window now. When it's closed it will be as good as a lead seal and everything will go back to normal. The town will be able to quit quivering and go back to sleep, with its paw over its nose.

I jump down, slam the window and look at Ralf. He is sitting on the bed, dishevelled, hapless, with his mouth open. For just an instant I feel ashamed of my antics. I suppose he hasn't treated me all that badly. In fact, as I put my clothes back on I feel almost motherly towards this thirty-year-old infant in his expensive suit who has just been given a good spanking. Our little talk is not finished yet, however. Oh-oh, Ralf is coming out in white blotches.

"It's over," I say with a smile. "Good-bye."

But now he is demanding explanations, squealing at me. The danger has passed, the stakes are no longer so high. It's time for him to put this crazy Russian woman in her place. I've bruised his ego, big time, and he is about to retaliate, proportionately of course. Proportionately and within the limitations imposed by his cowardice. He may try to give me a slap, or smash the lamp against the wall. No, he's scared to do even that. He's just going to yell and jump up and down, clench his fists and spray spit everywhere. I need to understand this, I need to do that, I don't know how lucky I am... Yeah, yeah, sweetie pie. Ja, Ja. I slam the door behind me.

As I come out I am feeling a lot taller than my evident one meter seventy. It's a wonder really that I didn't bang my head on the door frame. I press the elevator button and it lights up blue, as if some Russian Natasha, one eye coquettishly covered, is peeping out at me. I should be feeling victorious but for the moment don't. I am hearing no trumpet fanfares, my heart is not singing, and I need now to carry my victory quietly out of the block. I listen carefully, but behind Ralf's door all is quiet and a few seconds later I jump as the lift arrives. Serves you right, Ralf. You thought you could boss me about, but I decide things for myself, thank you very much. Always have. This speech I deliver to myself as this is an elevator with mirrors. I authenticate my official announcement with a thumbprint.

And yet, I do remember the wet hills of Paris, a city like a swing where we were constantly unbalancing the geometry of the streets, soaring up and into churches, swooping down and into Arab shops until, pleasantly wearied, we would sit in a cafe and talk about the future. That was about all you could do with Ralf at that time, because he was just starting up his big investment project. For the first time in my life I was making good money and reveling in the doors it opened, my freedom, and the frankly admiring way he looked at me.

As I came out on to the street I ran straight into a policeman, accompanied by a spry old man who was expatiating very loudly about something through his gray mustache. They both eyed me appraisingly but were about to let me pass when the old man pointedly tapped the policeman's sleeve.

"Excuse me. Was that you just now climbing out of the window?"

I had to turn around, and in some perplexity asked him to repeat the question.

"There was a naked woman up on the fourth floor for several minutes who appeared to be about to jump. Was that you?" The policeman frowned, trying to look serious.

"Yes, that was me, but if I'd been intending to jump I wouldn't have come down in the elevator."

Pause. The officer pondered how to categorize my behavior and whether to classify me as a victim or an offender. We stood motionless in front of the entrance to the apartments. I was already out in the street and the cars behind me were under starter's orders from the traffic lights to head over the bridge and disappear into the tentacles of the old district. If they hadn't been making so much noise, we would have been able to hear violins from the house opposite.

"Were you forced to do it?"

"No, I chose to do it entirely of my own free will."

"Why was that?"

"For personal reasons." I wanted an end to this idiotic dialogue, to go away and hide under the blanket of our little Russian courtyard where the buildings sprout satellite dishes like honey mushrooms.

"Are you a prostitute?" he asked, reacting to my accent.

"You wanna buy?"

"May I check your ID?"

He copied my details into his notebook. Passers-by glowered suspiciously at our little ensemble. Nothing ever happens on the streets around here, apart from people coming home or going out, and drinking cloudy young wine at kiosks. I raised my eyes and wondered what I must have looked like in that row of windows. The old man who had called the police must have thought he'd lost his marbles. There I was in the middle, looking as if I'd decided to hook on the concrete and glass building like butterflies' wings. Or perhaps just looking silly and pathetic. Who cares? I had taught my target audience its lesson.

"This is a disgrace," the old man said in the local dialect. "In front of children, in front of everybody. Go back to your country. You can do there whatever you please. They have no idea who they give passports to nowadays!" he expostulated, noticing my green passport in the police officer's hands.

"Stuff it!" I said, feeling all my contempt for this nation of smug sausage makers boiling up in me again. They have no soul, no feelings, and all they want is for everything to be the way they like it. They have scrubbed their towns into a state of total impersonality. No children play in them (they don't have children), you never hear people laughing, and at nine at night the whole lot of them, bang on cue, scuttle off to hide in their burrows behind lowered blinds, only to get up in the morning and with the same inhuman look of concentration crawl out of their houses and off to their jobs.

The police officer looked up from his notebook at us just as Ralf appeared behind him, his hair combed, his composure recovered, suave. I felt my face redden. He needed only a couple of seconds to take in the situation and slip past us to his Mercedes parked round the corner. Yes, it would be Ralf crowing now, if he wasn't too afraid of getting drawn into scandal. On reaching the corner he did summon up the courage to surreptitiously show me his middle finger. I'd had enough! I grabbed my Ausweis from the policeman as he was tucking his notebook away and flounced off, heedless of the old man's indignant cries.

"Come upstairs with us!" the policeman shouted after me.

"Sorry, must fly," I responded. I had no time because I have better things to do with my life than spend it in the midst of all these stage sets and low-fat foods. Better things to do than spend it with you, Ralf. Some other time in some other place, maybe, but right now it's time for me to leave. Don't beat yourselves up about it, sausage makers. For fifteen years I have lived in Germany. God is my witness how hard I tried to learn the language, to become German. What happiness it seemed not to stand out in the crowd, to go shopping without attracting attention, but then I found that all the German language is fit for is talking to shop assistants. Love and pain, death and happiness and disappointment have been monopolized by the Russians, leaving only longevity, hypocrisy, pettiness and vegetables labeled "organic" to the Germans.

I ran across the street and heard a veritable orchestra of violins. On the other side the policeman was still talking to the old man. They both looked pretty pathetic. Finally, they parted and I noticed that, although they were covering the ground at different rates, both were marching in time to the music coming from the windows.

MARK

Do you remember how my words were falling like burnt leaves, until all that was left was bare branches?

We had talked on the phone for several hours, and before we said goodbye you asked me to tell you something more before you went to bed, some last, beautiful thing, about love. You warned me you wouldn't be able to reply because you would be cleaning your teeth, only you did all the same reply, sounding funny with your mouth full of mint-flavored toothpaste. I pictured you standing in front of the mirror with your eyebrows raised, like a child who is just pretending to be talking on the phone, and I know you were enjoying looking at yourself. Bare feet enjoy losing themselves in the soft strands of a bathmat all the more because of the awareness that underneath are horrid cold tiles. Into that forest of warmth which has sprouted who knows how on the hard white surface, I alone can accompany you, Your Majesty's storyteller.

That evening I was on a roll. A little barque, filled with your voice, a receiver hot with your hands and your breath, sailed to every nook and cranny of my cramped apartment. I was just afraid the battery would run out at the wrong moment and I would not have time to draw everything to a close. Something of me would not have been decanted into you and would be left rattling like the seeds in a dried out pumpkin wherever I went. I sat down on the couch, filled my lungs with breath, but then you started talking again:

"Oh, my God," you say, pronouncing the words slowly, dismayed, "how awful I look."

Now's the moment. Now, only now:

"I know now that you are the love of my life."

I hear a barely audible rustling; you're brushing your teeth, looking pensively in the mirror but not at yourself, sideways, at the towels, leaving the rest of the space to spin as it will. Christine, my guiding star, my destiny, spit out all that mint-flavored gunk. I am saying to you something I have never said to anyone before. I want to kiss your tingling mouth and smear mint toothpaste all over your lips and cheeks.

"That's why all my life I've been repelling girls, girls who liked me, girls I liked. I would be walking alongside them trying to think what to talk about next, just as long as it wasn't what I was feeling in my heart of hearts."

You start to take an interest. Some siren inside you raises your attention level and, distorting the words through the toothpaste, you say something like, "And do you orrays te-ww mee hot you are fearing in yo heart of hearts?"

Even with your mouth full, I can hear the edge in your voice. Just as children collect seashells, so you exact your tribute of compliments from us. You glue your self-image together from what men tell you. Yes, that is a sign of weakness, but who am I to criticize? And what am I do? If that's what you want, I will give you yourself. Enjoy! I will pronounce you, express you, sculpt you, if you will just give me the commission. You keep a diary. It would not surprise me if you list the compliments paid to you with a note of the source and the circumstances. When I die I will be reduced to the things I am saying to you today, blue letters, painfully huddled in prickly paper snow next to today's date.

"Yes," I reply. "It is very easy, because before you I don't think anything ever happened in my heart."

Where did you find the key to the empty spaces inside me? To the secret cubbyholes, lumber rooms and cellars. I am not stupid. I know there is only one way you could have found it, and that is if I gave you it myself. When? Where? I don't know. I know only that it was my own choice and that all I can do now is hold on to it for dear life.

"The love of my life." Those words came to me last night. I seemed to be swimming, bursting up to the surface when I ran out of air. I woke every ten minutes. Exactly as now, I was talking to you and the water was whispering and laughing using your voice. Then I was washed up on a shore and, crawling, crashed headfirst into a rock on which your name was carved. Beneath it I found an inscription: "The Love of My Life". What was I to do? I sat down on the sand and laughed. It's you. My God, what happiness!

"Don't you have any regrets that the love of your life is quite like me?" You were rinsing your mouth, making room for ancillary questions so you could go to sleep with all the "i"s dotted, and sleep soundly and sweetly. "I'm not ideal. I'm impressionable and fickle." (Water splashing.) "It's not easy being with me. I..." You sound like someone deciding which dress to wear for the evening, "... am full of contradictions!"

For better or worse, I have been made just for you.

"You are saying such nice things to me, even rather serious, and I... am looking at myself in the mirror in horror. What a tired-looking face!" You run your fingers over your skin, smoothing out folds and faults only you can see.

Tired face or not, you are quite pleased with how you look, especially while I'm making my bumbling declaration of love. Your face and my words complement each other perfectly. You fit your tired body into the frame of my words. Overnight they will set and then never fit anybody else. Only you. Tomorrow morning you will see you are swaddled in my words, like a baby.

I live on the thirteenth floor. During the day you can just make out from my balcony the transparent heap of skyscrapers in Frankfurt. They must be thirty kilometers away. Closer, there are fields and, closer still, the city, like an overgrown flowerbed. You can tell where the Rhine is from the absence of streetlamps. If you want to look down, you have to go over to the window; from my divan I can see only sky. Right now there is no sky and I have no idea where it has gone. There is no sign of it, just blackness. I look up there. I have been wrung out and emptied. I have been pumped out, like the sky, but inside, in the vacuum, a crystal hammer is tapping. It is joy. All that is needed is to attach a tube and inside a valve will open through which love can pour into me.

Flop-flop-flop. Bare feet walk over the lino. She's put down the receiver. In the bathroom the mirror has misted. In the washbasin there are drops of water and flecks of toothpaste. The water will evaporate by morning, leaving the flecks. Good night, Christine, Christine, Chri...

VALERIA

I started writing because I had nothing better to do. Before that, my days were like sheets of lined paper in a school exercise book: I never got enough sleep, never had time to visit my parents. Now they are like sheets of paper in a sketchbook. It is autumn. In the streets you feel as if you are in a crate of oranges and I often remember school in Russia, the illustrations full of yellow autumn leaves at the end of the literature textbook. During the final exams, a couple of months ago, I left my job with a consultancy firm. I wanted to devote myself full time to finishing university.

I've got my degree now but there's no point in looking for a job. I've decided I'm moving to Moscow.

It all started about a year ago. I was working at an economics conference. The title included the word "dialogue", or perhaps it was "colloquium" or "symposium". Because I know Russian I was assigned to the Russian delegation and during one of the "dialogues" I met a Russian businessman from a major gas corporation. We just happened to be sitting next to each other at lunch. He looked weary and had the slightly irritated look of someone who'd been taken away from more important matters. I liked that. It meant he was not a professional chatterbox swanning around the world, but a grafter. He was a big man, huge even, little short of two meters tall. This made his bored appearance even more impressive, as if a bear had been brought to watch a featherweight boxing match. Oddly enough, his business suit looked good on him. He probably just told it to sit the way he wanted. He seemed to have an ocean of willpower. At the same time, there was nothing odd about Mr Gas. He didn't look like some out-of-place bird which had flown from the Siberian taiga. He had every right to be there, although he was funny too. I remember him muttering, "Here you're running errands. I've got girls your age heading departments."

We were sitting in a hotel bar with just the subtlest hint of the orient in its decor: a Taj Mahal on the wall and colorful drapery behind the rows of bottles. And him, huge and animated and sitting with a glass of something green and non-alcoholic. I have no idea now what kind of crap they drink in Moscow. He was heatedly trying to persuade me to come back home to Russia and, if the arguments were not all that convincing, his voice, full of energy, of passion even, was swaying me. If he had invited me up to his room with equal ardor I would't have gone, but I would at least have considered it, despite his age, his weight and his beard. I wasn't so much listening to him as just feeling amazed at the situation. Here I was, on the whole quite a smart cookie, sitting next to a huge man who was trying to persuade me to abandon everything and take off to a similarly huge country which simply couldn't do without me, and meanwhile I was staring at a wall with a picture of a white church which looked like a sugar shaker.

The weirdness of the situation was brought home when his secretary came running over to say my companion was long overdue at a meeting with the regional Finance Minister.

"I'll be right out. The capitalist can wait a bit longer," he replied, continuing his peroration on the subject of my Russian soul and the faults of Europeans. It hardly seemed likely that my returning to Russia would bring him any great kudos, while being late for such an important "dialogue" might well impact negatively on his career. Yet there he stayed, talking to me until his apoplectic secretary, waving his arms in the air, started turning the air blue with his swearing. This apparently over-the-top concern for my soul got me thinking that there must be more at stake here than a mere change of domicile. Some genetic memory gave me a sense of recurrence: my German ancestors had been summoned to Russia in much the same way, and they had dropped everything and gone. History seemed to be repeating, with Russia again needing Germans. This was again our time, and something deep inside me was responding. I would have liked not to care, but I couldn't.

Grim-faced people are boarding slippery black ships covered in green seaweed. There's something haphazard about it. They are certainly no proud column as they depart from their muddy northern port. Waves slap against the side of the ship like men's hands on women's bodies. The women wipe their eyes, but the men are focused: through the sea salt they smell damp earth which has never felt the touch of iron. These people were peasants, Bauern, not needed by anyone except tax collectors and those who sent them away to slaughter each other. Then men arrived from the recruiting offices of the Empress of Russia and they, still smeared with clay, felt they had substance. The land in Russia was suffering with no one to husband it. The steppes there were as boundless as the sky, and in all likelihood everything was topsy turvy and the sky was like water in a well; shout and it would shout back to you. We won't be dragooned into the army there. We'll be able to establish our language, our homes and our God. Everyone will forget about us and we will forget about them, out there on the Volga, unsere Wolga.

"Come back," he urged me. "When you finish your studies, I'll personally ensure everything goes well for you if you put your back into it, as no doubt the Fritzes have taught you to."

I am to return to Russia, to the land where generations of my ancestors lived out their lives. There I shall remember how they approached their task because I am, after all, a German, or at least, German blood flows in my veins. I can do anything. The land will yield. It will yield up its gas and we shall deliver it to every corner of the Earth. We shall feed that blue flame to the world, like milk to a soft-lipped calf.

My father likes to say I am German in every line of my ancestry. If you brought together all my forebears since they settled in Russia there would be a whole shipload, a shipload of Snow Germans, as I like to call them. They knew better than anyone how to manage the Russian land, all the while speaking their own language. My parents belong to the first generation for whom Russian was their native tongue, even though we had lived in Russia for two hundred years. We lived behind a wall, gave birth to children, vanished into the steppes, built white houses, and even painted the pigsties white. Now I'm all that remains of their lives, the only trace. There are no Volga German villages, no towns, not even any kindly memory of them. Today I'm all that can reunite them, even though they know nothing of my existence. Their ship sails by, the Snow Germans standing on its deck, looking out at the coast where I sit wearing a woolen dress my mother knitted. My face is covered by my hands and the Germans are silent.

I'm only twenty-six but have already gone back too many times for one life. There have been too many injunctions from forebears which I have had to or have yet to honor, as if it were they moving me hither and thither from country to country, like a figure on a chessboard or an African witch-doctor. First, it was needful for me to go back to Germany. Why me? It was as if my destiny was to give birth to the first baby who would have forgotten its roots, as if they were waiting, after all those generations of Germans, for a Russian child to be born.

My great-grandmother was Augusta. I am told she was strange. After giving birth to her third daughter, things would sometimes be revealed to her in visions and sometimes she would come out with weird, unexpected utterances. My grandmother, Augusta's daughter, told me that in the late 1930s the old lady begged her husband to emigrate to Canada or Paraguay or anywhere, as if she had a presentiment of all the calamities that were to follow. She was literally just five years too late: by that time nobody was being allowed to leave the Soviet Union. The family lived in Ukraine, in a German colony which was close enough to the border for the Russians not to have time to deport them at the beginning of the war before the Nazis arrived. Her husband had been arrested a couple of years earlier, and Augusta with her three daughters went out to see jubilant people welcoming the German tanks. The Snow Germans came as a surprise to the German Germans. After the famine, the dispossession of the prosperous "kulak" peasants, the closing down of churches, they were able once again to feel they had substance.

The people who lived in German villages did not believe that Germans could be bad people, but the new arrivals started rounding up their young men into police units, made them wear red arm bands, and took them off to hunt for Jews and partisans in the neighboring forests. It was then the Bauern discovered that it was not only in Russia that madmen had come to power. They were not asked which side they wanted to be on in the war. All they wanted was to be left in peace but they were not asked, any more than those Snow Germans who lived further from the border and whom there was time to deport to Siberia and Kazakhstan. They were scooped up indiscriminately.

Well, I was writing about going back. We have a family legend that Augusta prophesied at that time that we would return to Germany. "But not now," she said. "We will go back not as the result of war, but of peace." Her listeners said nothing. What was there to say? She was probably right. Everything was as plain as it had been in the late eighteenth century when they left Germany because to live there had become impossible. At that time, it was not even Germany, just a lot of tiny principalities. Fathers assembled their unprotesting families, drinking their soup. Yes, of course we must, so go we shall. It was the same in the early 1990s when the Snow Germans were preparing to go back to Germany; they took the decision in just the same way. Of course we must go, of course. The soup was getting cold. My mum saw pictures some relatives sent of the inside of a German maternity hospital, and often said that with conditions like that in Germany she would have another baby, a boy for dad. That was the clincher for me too: of course I had to go, my little brother was there waiting for me. It was obvious. He was as tiny as a pea, he hadn't yet even been born, but already he was as lively and happy as a sandboy.

We went back, but I didn't get my brother.

I learned almost by accident what befell Augusta later. For some reason my family was reluctant to talk about this, although I find it wonderful and almost incredible. A German patrol detained a Jew in the street. My great-grandmother and her daughters Else, Inge and Lise were just passing. He suddenly broke away and ran up to her, begging for help. He was trying to persuade the men in grey uniforms that he was Armenian and asked Augusta to confirm this and assure the patrol she was an old friend of his. She did so and, with some regret, they released him. That night the Jew, whose name was Yefim, came to their house to thank her. Augusta found some food for him and a little money, and in the early morning he went off to join his own people in the forests.

Later in the war, Soviet troops were advancing and the Nazis, as they were leaving, evacuated the Snow Germans with them. The trains bearing them westwards departed without panic and in strict accordance with a timetable. There was obviously no choice but to leave. "We will not be brought back to Germany by war," August continued to insist. The Snow Germans were assembled in Poland. Young German girls were given good-quality, warm clothing to wear, which had most likely been confiscated from murdered Jewish girls. The Red Army liberated Poland and the Snow Germans were crammed into cattle cars and sent off to the east.

Inge, Augusta's middle daughter, did not survive the weeks of journeying in appalling conditions and died on the way. My grandmother told me her mother had always been especially kind and gentle to Inge even before she fell sick. I believe she knew what was going to happen. I have no children and can't imagine what she must have felt. I shan't even attempt to write about it.

That gas businessman did not know my family history when he urged me to return to Russia. I remembered, though, that the Germans too disappointed us in the war. People were waiting eagerly, or at least hopefully, for them to arrive, my grandmother told me. They disappointed us again in the 1990s.

In Germany we Russian Germans call the natives "pure" Germans: he is a pure German, while I am a Russky. It's because the snow melted off the Snow Germans. For as long as we had the snow, we were Germans, but when it melted we were already Russkies. Beneath the snow we had been slowly changing. Even so, there is something German inside us that cannot be washed away.

The Snow Germans were deported to a large city in the Urals. Only two of Augusta's daughters had survived, but they and their mother were separated from all the others almost immediately. The rest were packed off to labor camps to fell timber and build factories. The officials had found out that Augusta's husband had been arrested, which made her doubly criminal. A case was opened against her too, but while they were rooting through their archives to decide how to classify her she was under less strict surveillance and, while being moved between prisons, in temporary accommodation at a railway station, she was able to squeeze Lise and Else out of a small window to freedom. "To their deaths," the other women in the cell told her. "Du bist wohl verrückt," they cried. Even a Soviet children's home would be better than death.

I picture the girls, Lise eleven and Else just eight years old. They are walking along a road with frozen puddles in those warm, brightly coloured German coats they had been given in Poland. The fat women coming towards them in quilted jackets or wrapped in rags look askance at them. They meet cripples who have lost legs, beggars, soldiers, pale evacuees. It is cold and they are terribly frightened. It is 1945. In the distance they can hear the rumbling of factories. The Germans had advanced so quickly there had been no fighting, and three quiet years had followed. They had been in well-provisioned Ukraine, then in well-provisioned Poland. For the girls the war only began when Soviet troops arrived. Before that there was just their childhood.

They started to encounter workers' barracks along the road. The girls had been going hungry for a month and decided to ask for food but, not speaking Russian, asked in German and Polish. The people in the first hostel gave them bread, but those in the second and third sent them on their way. They decided to knock on one last door before going off into the forest, from which they would probably never have emerged. They knew from fairy tales that nothing bad ever happens to German girls in forests. When they knocked, however, it was Yefim who came out to the porch, the Jew whose life Augusta had saved. After a few months he had been able to contact his people and had ended up in the Urals working as an engineer in a factory.

Yefim did not recognize them, but Lise recognized him. She never forgot that patrol and his terrified lamentations. Yefim took them in. That night he wept, rolling around like a badly trimmed log. He gave up his bed to the girls and himself slept on the floor. A few days later he managed to buy a certificate to the effect that Lise and Else were the children of his sister who had been killed by the Nazis. His sister had really existed and so had her children, but not only two, and they had all really been murdered. He gave the girls new names, talked to them in Yiddish, and gradually taught them Russian. They did not see much of him, because Yefim went off to his factory in the morning and returned late at night, and meanwhile the girls stayed home as quiet as mice. Two years passed like that. Yefim saved up his money and thought of returning to the Ukraine. He acquired a house on the coast and then a plump wife with a black mole near her lip, a new mother for his daughters. It was then that the most extraordinary, and also the last, miracle in our family history happened.

The miracle was that, after two years, Augusta was released from her prison camp. As far as I can tell, this wholly exceptional outcome was related to the fate of her husband, who seems somehow to have been able to affect it. How, and whether indeed he was alive by then, I have no idea. He never returned from the camps.

Great-grandmother was not even conscripted into the labor army, although she was compelled to sign a statement repudiating any claim to property confiscated from her, and any right to return to the Ukraine. Augusta was given a job in the administration of a village in northern Kazakhstan but, on her way there, found herself beside the very window through which she had pushed her little ones. She set off in their footsteps. I have no doubt in my mind she would have marched purposefully straight to the hostel and the split-level room on whose floor Yefim slept while Else and Lise slept in the bed. I picture her heading there without doubts, without stopping, without knocking or shouting out the names of her daughters to the neighbors. It is just something I know.

Else saw her from the window, screamed, jumped up and down, and ran through the stale air of the communal corridor, afraid she was only imagining it. She almost went back to the window to check, but instead got to the door and ran outside. She was in such a hurry to hug her mother she knocked her over and the two of them fell to the ground. Lise came scampering behind and the two of them bore their mother back into the hut like an injured bird; to their room, to their bed, to their secret hideaway, in haste, inside before anyone would see them; away from the war and the prison, the cattle cars and timber-felling, the red stars and swastikas, Hitler and Stalin, guards and frozen clothing.

Forty years later, Else had a granddaughter, and here I now am.

I exchanged e-mails with my gas man and, only too accustomed to knocking on every door, sent him my resume, just in case. Of course! Come! You are just who we need, was his reply. I responded that I had to finish my studies. "How much longer do you have to go?" he enquired. I would be graduating in August but, just for luck, threw in the fall. "February, then," he emailed. Until February he was going to be somewhere around the Gulf of Finland supervising the laying of pipes on the seabed, or so I understood. "Fine," I replied. "What about the job title, salary, and job description?" He replied to that too. It was a bit more than I might have expected in an American or German business. I found the image of pipelines at the bottom of the sea, streaming that blue energy to Europe, quite heart-warming. It was as if a new circulatory system was being created and that there, in Russia, the great heart of the world was beating. Soon its throbbing would reach Germany and its warm blood would wake the somnolent sausage makers, the cities would give themselves a good shake, and people would find their eyes were full of love. It was time for me to make up my mind.

MARK

People who count the weeks in terms of supermarket promotions believe that love is something ethereal and elusive. At best they imagine it as the scent of perfume, the lingering fragrance in an elevator of the woman who ascended in it last night, practicing words which in the end she had no occasion to say. They are wrong, of course. I see my love for you very clearly, sometimes even with my eyes open. It is a blue flame some 20-30 centimeters tall which comes out of my chest, from my heart I think, although I can't be sure. It flickers like a candle flame in time to my breathing, my pierced ribcage aches, and my body is confused and quiescent. I lie on my back naked, woven into a cover as smooth as a candy wrapper, and make love to you.

Yesterday at the rail station, as I was plowing my way through all the escalators, platforms, underground passages, malls with Chinese diners, McDonaldses, fast seafood restaurants, the information queue, the ticket machines, and more escalators, I detected your reflection a thousand times, concealed in this labyrinth. Smiling, hiding behind a concrete partition, you were following me from two steps away; you were there as I went into a newsagent's to look for my article; you were walking briskly away over the tramlines in the street, lit by the light from kebab shops where Turkish and Arabic could be heard, and unshaven men wearing gold chains clicked their tongues as you passed. Christine, tired and fretful in a long, slow train; Christine, vivacious, catching the light from the station lamps, from screens and push-buttons; Christine the juggler, making the light spin round your slender legs; Christine out of sorts, with people respectfully making way to provide an empty corridor in which, like autumn leaves, used tickets and advertising brochures yellow and curl on tables. My small, dear girlfriend, teach me how not to be jealous every time you mention a male name.

Then at last I saw you and all the Christines merged into one, molded instantly into the solid you, your voice, your smell, your white jacket. I bumped into someone as I rushed to close the space between us, and of course failed to apologize, as you promptly remarked. Your hair has become darker – only three more steps – you have two bandaged fingers. "Oh, hello! I'm so happy to see you!"

A little later we were walking up the path to my lofty high-rise which sticks out like a Tower of Babel. We walked past dark, damp, chaotically stirring bushes, past the fence of the swimming pool, which is closed until next summer. I was agitated. Those first few minutes of our date seemed overly meaningful, as if our every touch carried some mysterious significance, every word spoken altered the rhythm of my breathing. It had been too long, more than a week, since I'd seen you, and I just couldn't keep up that cool tone of voice I was so proud of when we spoke on the phone. The absence of passersby, the tawdry brown light falling from the street lamps, the hue of your suntanned body seemed to be authorizing me to act with less restraint, but I did nothing to bring forward our intimacy. I meekly led you by the hand, and you chose to say nothing.

We said nothing in the elevator either. It would have been silly to pretend we did not know what should be going to happen, and it did not yet seem time to start the game. "There," I thought, "a man is leading his woman to bed. His girl. That's how it's supposed to be." But somehow I knew you were not in a great mood. I was afraid to ask what was wrong in case that disrupted the proceedings, the schedule of the happy evening I'd so been looking forward to. Lately you had not been seeing me often. The elevator was taking a hundred years, humiliating me with every unwanted second. I could not dispel the awkwardness, and then the whole apartment block shook as the doors opened.

Suddenly everything came right. Just when I was about to give up, something flared between us and burst into flames. I poured the Greek wine, then kissed your newly Greek lips. You were scattering sequins of light like pollen wherever I found your shiny blouse, until I took it off and it curled up and fell asleep like a cat. The world disappeared, the light disappeared and, wiping its feet, the wet autumn disappeared. The skyscrapers of Frankfurt outside disappeared, the wind turned to water, the stairs collapsed like dominoes, the elevator sank down into the basement, the second hands stitched the night to fit us perfectly. Ten minutes later the world came back, the cat screeched, the doorbell rang. Irascible, wearing whatever I had pulled on, I told a person unknown where he could stuff his absurd commercial offer. You were laughing. "You should have told him straight out you had a naked girl in bed and he would have vanished immediately."

You had only to click your fingers and I too would have disappeared.

Afterwards I found my jeans and went out to the balcony because I felt too hot. The town was growing down below, an unruly, firefly bicycle lamp flickered and buzzed as it approached my feet. A sock impacted on the half-open balcony door. "Shut it! I'm cold!" you shouted, miming someone sitting on an ice floe. I shut it and was alone.

There are a lot of trees here. On windy days the city rolls in towards my windows in waves. You could believe you lived at sea. Directly beneath me are the two-story buildings of our University's fine arts department. Sometimes the lights stay on in there till late. The artists are covering their canvases with paint. As I pass by I try to glimpse the paintings through the huge window but can make out neither form nor content. Apart from the artists, all you meet here are squirrels and residents of other apartments. Through our buildings is the quickest way down to the town.

A little beyond the treetops is the vast area of an outdoor swimming pool, which lies where it is like a dark swamp until May, except that in the corner an indoor pool is open all year round and glows like a translucent blue crystal. I recollect swimming in its blue core a few days ago and the flame from my chest mingled with the color of the water and I seemed to be swimming in love, scooping it with my hands so it flowed through my fingers into me and became me. The recollection gives me an instant, acute attack of longing for you which takes my breath away. I hold this feeling inside me, not letting it go, enjoying the prospect of instant relief because I'll see you as soon as I go back into the room.

Suddenly I feel fear, fear that you will never come

to see me again. My situation is, after all, precarious. I'm walking a high wire of telephone cable. Perhaps the sex is only my payment for entertaining you.

After the fear I feel rage. Why? Why is it like this? Why so little? How can it not be obvious that we are made for each other. You must be blind not to see it. You are not giving me enough, Christine! It is too little because you won't admit the obvious, that we need to hold on to each other. The balcony door clicks. You have crept over, locked it, and now you are pulling scary faces at me through the glass. I'm stranded on the balcony, already very cold but also grimacing, my face distorted by pain and fear. For a while we continue making faces at each other, until I lose patience and beat on the plastic partition. You pretend to be terribly frightened. Let me in, Christine. You roll your eyes comically, left and right, pressing your hand to your lips. I give in and burst out laughing, but at the same time tears begin to flow. My face is still twisted, my mouth open, only a scary mask. Oblivious of everything, you scamper back to the bed, under the quilt, and peep out slyly, your little fists under your chin.

Let me in, Christine. I'm cold. I'm being nibbled at from the back by squirrels, the leaves are peeling my skin off, the light from the street lamps is boring through me. Or perhaps you'd better not let me in. I'm afraid I may have been possessed by some evil force, and God only knows what I might say. I will beg you to move in and live with me here, to be warm, to sleep with the radiator turned on. It starts its knocking at 5.00 a.m. precisely. You will wake up and turn over on to your other side. I'm afraid I may start pleading with you. I may tell you about the blue flame, and the swimming pool full of love. For heaven's sake, that is complete nonsense and I must keep it to myself.

You opened the door, and I really did tell you God knows what. You asked me to wait a moment, clambered over me on the bed, not as you might over someone you loved, but mechanically, like a Jeep driving over a sand-dune. You immediately took your mobile phone and went into the bathroom.

When you came back you had changed, as if the Christine you saw in the mirror had told you something bad about me, quietly and emphatically, and then had laughed and sent someone else a text message. Or perhaps you changed places, and now the real Christine will always live in my mirror, and the one who is leaving so carefully, trying not to put pressure on her bandaged fingers, but swiftly, too swiftly buttoning up her jacket, the one kissing me goodbye and telling me everything was great, is the stranger from the mirror. I wish I knew who it is I love, the you who has just left or the you who is still lying here with me, like a cloud's shadow on my candy wrapper duvet on the thirteenth floor since the birth of Christ.

VALERIA

It's too ridiculous! Everything has turned out in the stupidest way imaginable. The old man who called the police the day I climbed out of the window naked, that silly old fart I argued with in the street, decided to prosecute me for causing a disturbance in a public place. He claimed he was walking in the street that evening with his family and the sight of me so disturbed his granddaughter that she cried all night and couldn't go to school the next day because she was just too upset. By way of evidence he produced a doctor's certificate and made enough copies of it to leaflet half the town. I turned up at the hearing, took one look at the old man (odd I hadn't noticed any impressionable granddaughters with him that evening), Ralf, summoned as the landlord of the premises with the ill-starred window, and the judge. I was thoroughly rude to everyone and ran off to the park to stamp on the leaves. I tried not to think about their stupid hearing, ran a few circuits, wore down my running shoes a bit, and mused that summer is a real fire, while fall is like when it is being put out, and there is endless rain and the air in your nostrils smells a bit like after a fire.

A few days later I pulled the court adjudication out of my mailbox. Wrapped around it was a cheesy pizza advert which looked as if it might be dripping butter. I was to pay a fine and court costs, which all added up to just over a thousand Euros. These last few months I've felt as if Germany just wanted to throw me out, as if I was back to being the white crow again, as if Germany had declared war on me. Just hold off for a couple of months, can you? Come February I'll leave you and there will be nobody to disturb your mental equilibrium and your windows can stay closed for the rest of time. To draw a line under the piece of nonsense, I called a law student I know and carefully, without going into details, asked him whether appearing naked in public was such a heinous crime. He explained that, although there was nothing intrinsically illegal about it, a lot depended on the law of the Land government, what mood the judge was in, and the details I'd said I did not want to divulge. The conversation trailed off into small talk and, needless to say, as soon as I hung up, Ralf phoned to have a gloat. I came close to throwing the phone out the window (which would doubtless have cost me a thousand and a half, because I know for a fact there's a dumb law prohibiting such delinquency). I felt sorry for myself, and at the same time angry I'd wasted so much time on a man who had such a pathetic, sniggering little soul inside him.

I had no choice but to pay up, spending the money that I'd been saving for almost a year to live on during and after my exams and for moving to Moscow. On the way back from the bank it occurred to me I should look for a job. Nothing serious, just for a couple of months, to make ends meet. I would get out of the apartment perhaps a couple of times a week and it seemed unlikely to adversely affect my self-improvement phase, as I was calling my inactivity between now and February. The Frankfurt firm I'd been working for the last couple of years would have been glad to have me back, but that was not what I wanted. I'd left that job, I told them about my Russian offer, and my colleagues toasted my future with champagne. In any case, I wanted a break from finance and computers and wearing business clothes.

There was a documentary on television that evening about the River Ganges, and from my speakers a melody uncoiled as unhurried as Arabic script and braided into long tresses. It put me in mind of the hotel bar where a conversation had opened the prospect of returning to Russia and I thought I might as well work for a couple of months as a waitress. The idea cheered me up instantly and I even bounced up and down on the sofa in time to the music. I practiced saying with different intonations, "What would you like for your main course?" and "What will you drink?" It was just what I needed: minimal responsibility and the opportunity to glide like a ghost between people without being part of the crowd. I would soon have tired of sitting at home all the time and, to cap it all, I could take a final close look at the Germans. As my grandmother used to say, it wouldn't wear my eyes out.

Ten years earlier I made my debut on the stage of life in a big beer tent at a fair. It was my first job and I whisked with my tray past grunting, prosperous men who raised fat fingers while they were giving an order. I felt like Snow White among the dwarfs. The long wooden benches were as packed as perches in a hen house. Old geezers announced with touching gravitas their wish for "Pils" or "Weizen" or "Dunkles", as if they were proclaiming the Constitution. Younger men sported long hair, a bushy mustache and knitted wrist bands, a fad of the time. They looked like ugly horses. I felt I was ethereal, floating, but later my legs really hurt. On the plus side, I earned a lot of money; people smiled and were pleased to see me. I was part of this world, part of the best of it, its elite, presumably. It was pink and airy. I soon tired of the feeling. Even then I was no airhead. It was just that for the previous four years, since moving to Germany, I had been in a state of dark depression.

I don't suppose it was anyone's fault that at the age of thirteen I was on my own, sent somewhere I didn't want to go, the butt of jokes, a stupid parrot which couldn't say anything, a piece of ass in red jeans and a green jacket wandering the streets of a gray town in East Germany. I can't blame the Germans or the Russians or my parents. I froze up inside and have ever since been as cold as the Antarctic. In order not to worry my parents, and just to have a life, to allow for the possibility that something might happen, I had to go out and meet people, encountering pity, sympathy, puzzlement, indifference and contempt: so much contempt it's taken me years to scrape it all off. I didn't want anything I didn't deserve, neither love nor admiration, only my due. I wanted to be seen for the pure, clever little girl I was, honest and hard-working. I wasn't asking for their pity or their sympathy, only that they should judge me fairly, no more than that.

It's not that people were cruel, it's just that the trials

which beset me were something only the future, highly competent Valeria could be expected to cope with. Instead I was lumbered with the Valya I had been in Russia, ill-prepared, naive, unsociable and ridiculously Russian. I was just waiting for the change to come, for my replacement to arrive and let me, as I was, go home to read my books and draw pictures in my rough book of myself riding on horseback and engaging in acts of valor. It took my replacement four years after the move to Germany to arrive, as I was whizzing around with beer mugs, catching the admiring glances of Germans, even if they were only noisy, harmless German pensioners. This new Valeria derived great satisfaction from being so out of their league. Within a few months she'd become the captain of the city's volleyball team, won a place at a good school, and boys were falling over themselves to ask her out on a date. At that point the former, worn-out little Valya put on the woolen dress her mother had knitted and the green jacket from the Red Cross and departed. She probably went back to Katya and now lives under her bed, hiding from the daylight behind a pile of books and dirty dishes. She will be pale now and covered with acne but as happy as can be, fervently kissing the kindly hand reaching down to her and asking nothing more. My little Valya, let me take a look at you... no, the distance between us is too great, so gallop away on a horse you have drawn until the laughing wind weeps cold tears for you.

Back then Valya's main regret had been that she'd miss the end of a film on TV. Part Two was being shown the following Friday and the flight to Germany was on Wednesday night. Her friend Katya came running round to say goodbye but for some reason wouldn't come inside. She stood on the landing, trembling, her hands tucked under her elbows, burst into tears and gave me, that is, Valya, of course, a letter and asked her not to open it before the plane took off. In those days before they left, the old Valya seemed to be sleepwalking. She was in a daze, constantly listening to herself, like listening in a seashell for the sea. Something was humming inside her, and she was calm and detached. She packed her belongings as if she were sending her doll off on a cruise. Not really, just a pretend one.

The city was buzzing with rumors that thieves were robbing Russian Germans the night before they left, knowing they would have sold all their belongings and have a lot of money on them. How secretively everyone packed! Mother made up stories to put her friends off the scent, and they went along with it, and watching the whole charade was unbearable. They said goodbye to everybody in an empty apartment, my father skipping about like a young boy, lean and nimble and with my mother shrieking and trying to join in but after a couple of moves suddenly crumpling and lumbering through to the next room as if she thought she was bumping into the furniture. There was something our guests were keeping quiet about. They hugged us and patted us, and did not mention something, as if there was a dead body next door which they had agreed not to talk about. People seemed mostly not to be saying anything, even when they were talking. How can I explain? Go on, Valeria, you're smarter than me. You can put it into words better than I can. Do you remember you tore off a piece of wallpaper as a keepsake? We had lived there such a long time, but then we just left and that was it. We vanished, dissolved like sugar in tea.

And do you remember that apartment, dusty and creaking, owned by some distant relatives, and you slept on a mattress and, going for a pee in the night, heard the lady of the house cursing us all under her breath for not having left them more stuff, and complaining that what little there was was rubbish they couldn't sell? That night you tried to count up all the things you had lost and couldn't because you had lost your entire universe, except for the soap operas which people said were just the same over there, only a couple of hundred episodes more recent. If you're giving up everything, how are you to tell what's going to seem most important later? What am I, your replacement, going to need from all the piles of junk? Your inner scales broke then. Everything got mixed up in a single heap, the movie you wouldn't see the end of, Katya, school, your home, the village, and Chernushka the Cow. They all went round on a roundabout, and you were being left behind too, because you were sure you would change the moment you got off the plane in Germany. In the morning you looked out the window and saw the city lying there like a sour apple someone had taken a bite out of before throwing it away, and your parents were on edge and shouting at each other, and then the car came and you all left for the airport.

In the plane you read Katya's letter. I've forgotten it already. All I remember is a single phrase: "For me our city will be empty without you."

Shall I go on? Coming down the steps from the plane, you thought you'd already changed, but when you were walking round the airport like a dog on a leash, trying not to lose sight of the meeting point where you were supposed to be collected by relatives who, for some reason, did not turn up; when your distraught parents urged you to ask somebody where you should go, since after all you had studied German at school, that's when you realized you had not changed, not one little bit, but still you went to break down the glass wall behind which you were wandering about, making no contact at all with those thousands of people speaking their incomprehensible language and passing by and almost through you. This was not your familiar Deitsch which quietly inhabited your grandparents' home, and not even your school German with its guttural "r" and solemnity of tone; it was a strange language you had never heard before, almost a noise, a sound like the rustling of leaves, which had not the least intention of breaking down into words. And of course, you remember the evening sun warming the chocolate-colored seats in the bus which you finally discovered, and thinking that at least the sun was the same here as ours. It was the only similarity you did manage to find.

And then there was Zörbig, a gray, moribund little town in East Germany: "It's like being back in Russia," Mother said. You were sent east almost immediately from Friedland, the first camp for migrants to which the bus with the chocolate-colored seats took you. What you remember of Friedland are the hundreds of people queuing for the canteen, the yogurts (which you explained to yourself as a mixture of sour cream and jam), the long, disappointing sausage squeezed into what looked like a shiny candy wrapper, and the supermarket doors which opened in front of you. You thought there was a man pulling a string to open them and didn't want to trouble him too often when you were only going in to look around. It seemed impolite. Yes, my dear, I feel like crying when I think what became of the young girl who felt sorry for the animals, and the mechanism, and the man operating the doors, but I will go on. In Zörbig Russian Germans were given the barracks left behind after Soviet troops withdrew: rooms with barred windows and bunk beds. You slept on a top one, and were woken in the morning and sent to school.

In Friedland there was a good Red Cross center, where new and secondhand clothes, toothbrushes and all sorts of other necessities were issued. Everybody agreed the Red Cross center in Zörbig was dire, and you ended up dressed like a clown or some absurd bird in clothes that didn't fit, were brightly colored, and looked terrible together. The weather was getting cold and you had to wear what you had. You were taken to school, as required by law, placed in one of the classes and left to your own devices. You sat all day in the back row and did the lessons in Russian school textbooks you brought because, of course, you could not understand what the teacher was saying. Every morning you passed like a spark along the empty streets lined with two-story buildings, which looked nothing like houses should. It was idiotic, terribly pointless going to school, sitting on your own and writing stuff in your Russian work book.

Your classmates had long ago given up on you. They couldn't even be bothered to bully you. The only ones who came over were those studying Russian. It was a kind of game, trying to sort out their "pidgin" Russian. Neither you nor they were capable of taking the conversation any further. Sometimes you were asked the meaning of a Russian word, but the words they didn't know in Russian, you didn't know in German, so that line of communication soon fizzled out too.

Who were you? An inmate of the school's pets' corner? An ugly, dumb but harmless animal? The pages of your work book were duly covered in even handwriting. I've kept them and they are still stacked in my parents' basement. When you got into your schoolwork, you imagined you were back at school in Russia and needed to quickly work out all the answers, raise your hand and go to the front of the class and speak out loudly and clearly. That was happiness, speaking, answering questions, and being awarded top marks of five, and pleasing your father. But then you'd look up to see the German children in front of you lounging about, a slight hum of talking going on in the class, a bored teacher walking to and fro in front of the blackboard. There was no soul in this, no sincerity, no excitement, no sense of success being rewarded. You could feel that, even without knowing the language. You again lowered your head to the book and again, into the old castle in which the Zörbig school was located and which occupied the space so absurdly, there stole that studious and spectral Russian school; corridors appeared with strict, bespectacled schoolmistresses walking down them who wore checkered clothing and sometimes cried in the teachers' room, homework books and classroom newspapers, "Good morning, children!" and the thunder of chairs being moved back when the teacher came into the classroom and everyone, even the worst students, stood up. You were the only pupil in that imagined Russian school, arriving in the morning, leaving in the afternoon, and everything else, even Germany itself, was no more than a stage set, a mock-up, the noise from a radio you don't want to listen to but which, as you can't turn it off, you learn to block out.

Father went to work for a farmer, on the side, secretly from the authorities, digging out his potatoes; mother's main occupation was trying to engineer our move westwards. When you came back from school you did your homework in your dark room, which resembled a train compartment, before clambering up to your bunk, under the ceiling, to watch TV and lie about, warming up and waiting for something to happen. In the evenings your room really did turn into a railway compartment, like the ones you traveled in all over Siberia selling knitted sweaters; you jerked your foot in time to the rhythm of the wheels and the horse-like quivering of the car. Do you remember how a moment would come when you felt a shunting and the barracks would move and slowly pull away towards the fields over which the suspended droplets of drizzle hovered like midges? It floated over the potatoes which Father was digging, along riverbanks and mountain ranges, and it was only the destination you were unable to imagine, because it was unthinkable to face the disgrace of going back to Russia without having achieved anything.

Two plump, harmless girls, who had been living in the barracks for several years now among all those beds of Soviet soldiers, took you one time to see a nun who had a children's club. You sang German Christmas carols and drank tea with unappetizing cookies you weren't even allowed to dunk in it to get rid of the horrid scraping sound the coarse granulated sugar made on your teeth. The nun was cloyingly sweet, smiled too much, and seemed dull and obtuse. Okay, that's my word, not yours. You have only to recall the way she was continually looking shortsightedly round at all of you with those doe-like eyes, and reading Bible stories for children in her cracked voice. Her apartment was full of old furniture. How stupid, you thought, to have so much stuff and none of it pretty. There was a Christmas tree in one corner, not a Russian one with colorful baubles, which could put even a zombie in the mood for Christmas better than any doll. No, this one had candies as hard as nuts, and fir cones. You discovered that Germans hang cones and wooden figures on their Christmas trees. What on earth for? The tree was already wooden. What fool doesn't know that?

Can you remember being taken by similar benefactors to McDonald's, and you asked them to spell the word out because you could not find it in the dictionary? Do you remember your worst fears were realized when one morning you woke to find your whole face covered with acne, so that it glowed as crimson as an eggplant and you had to comb your hair forward on to your cheeks? And what about when Mother finally managed to get permission to move to West Germany, and your parents told you that now you would see the real Germany, and you were staring out the window still in your red jeans with your equally red face and watching the Soviet-style districts of pre-fabricated buildings being replaced by lively little white towns, but you seemed no longer capable of feeling anything?

Changing where you lived and, more importantly, the school you went to, brought many changes for the better. For a start, you were no longer alone because there were four other Russian children in your class and one, Grisha, knew even less German than you and didn't seem the least bit bothered by the fact. He just sat there for days at a time, a big, tousled boy nobody was going to try to push around, looking out the window. Little Valentina was a Baptist, with incredibly long, braided hair tied in a great knot at her waist, which looked as if it could be swung like a mace and put paid to any taunting boy. Yakov was a quick, agile boy always running after the girls, even during Kochunterricht when you were learning to use pots and pans and cookers. And then there was pert, likeable Zhenia, for whom you'd later write hundreds of love letters which always began "My dearest Ivan..."

The German children were not much interested in what went on over there in the "Russian sector" of the class. The two worlds had almost no point of contact until you yourself violated the borders by starting to answer during lessons and getting better marks than they did, but that was still far in the future. For the present you were just beginning to understand what the teachers were saying. Do you remember you used to believe it was impossible to talk nonsense in German? Enlightenment came in a biology class. You were studying moss, and for a full forty-five minutes moss was all that was talked about. You had your suspicions at the time, and when at home with the aid of a dictionary you read the long section of the textbook devoted to this plant, you concluded it contained no serious information whatsoever. There were poems, funny stories, a large, full-page drawing, jokes, chatter, a dialogue between two hedgehogs and a song, but nothing like real knowledge, nothing that made you feel your reading had been worthwhile and that you now knew more about moss than you did before.

I see the classroom as two crystal spheres. We are sitting in one and the German children in the other. Sometimes the two impact on each other and then a light crystalline ping is heard, like when people clink glasses. All the rest of the space is overgrown with moss, dumb, fluffy German moss about which the only thing you can do is sing a song. Young Valya, I'll bring you as far as the day when you first gave an answer in class and leave you there. It was a history lesson about Ancient Greece, and the question was about Troy. The Brad Pitt movie had not yet been released, so only you knew the answer. When you put up your hand the class immediately fell silent. You began shaking. Two words were spinning around in your head: "Holz" and "Pferd". You somehow tied them together, muttered something, and the teacher growled encouragingly. He was entirely satisfied to find you knew anything at all about Troy.

Now let me tell you about me. I climb out of windows in the nude in order to infuriate a man I don't even love but who I've been sleeping with for the last few years. Here's another story, about school again. In the senior classes, everybody was going crazy over the boys in a pop group. I fancied one as well. He was called Nick. They come one time to our town and were performing right in front of the volleyball hall where we practiced. That day training was abandoned. Those girls who hadn't managed to get a ticket were hanging on the fence in front of the building where the concert was taking place. I was all alone in the echoing, empty hall, standing tall and proud. I punched the ball and it flew straight and smooth and trembling slightly like a taut string. Like birds the balls flew one after the other, and I thought, "No, Nick, I'm not one of your fans. I'll get to know you a different way." Do you know what? I'm certain that if I had not dropped the idea, I'd have had my way. I would have met him and gone on to marry him, I the girl from Siberia, the red and green parrot from the GDR, the school frump, the swot and know-all. There is nothing I could not have done, but now I am going back to Russia, and there I'll rise to the very top, and our pipelines will transport warmth all around the world, and our blue flame will be reflected in the moist eyes of grateful, loving people.

Stalingrad, 7 January 1943

My dearest Annie,

Tell me where you would like me to begin describing to you my cold, dark days, bright days, dark days, and again, and now forever, bright days. I worry for you and the children. The mail comes infrequently and with a great delay. That is really the only complaint I can address to

God. While we are encircled, all of our communication with the outside world is by air. You can send letters only by airmail. I am sending a special stamp for your reply. For the time being I have a lot of them because my comrades rarely write. There is not so much to write about. For several months now there has been no change in our positions. Everybody here dreams of Christmas parcels with cake and chocolate and ersatz honey. They have not yet been delivered. We are told it is not practical, and we survive on horse meat and bread, and drink melted snow. Many have given up hope, but not I. It is no easier for me than for anyone else yet my heart is full of joy in these cold steppes, and I want your heart to be just as joyful back home in Magdeburg, and to beat in time with mine. My darling, I have good news for you. You remember why I volunteered for the front? It was talked about on the radio, in the newspapers, the same words were posted up in every shop window and whispered by us as we were putting on the uniform and taking up our rifles. Now my rifle seems to have a life of its own. Sometimes it becomes hot, then cold again, and sometimes I wonder how I am connected with its life. My darling, all the reasons that caused me to end up here, let us simply call them The Great Idea, were lies and deceit. The Great Idea which lived in our hearts as we traveled in railway cars through the endless fields, clutching our weapons and happy, did not follow us down into the trenches, did not go with us into the attack, and left us abandoned when we came under artillery bombardment and, deafened, were then digging the dead out of the ground only to re-bury them in the same trenches. Occasionally, it flew in to visit us with generals who ordered reviews and parades, but soon I learned to recognize its true face and to see it was without substance, a ghost laughing at us, drinking and eating at our funerals, because The Idea has no interest in whether we win or lose this war, or whether we are killed out here and freeze solid until the spring when dogs which have gone wild dig up our bodies and pull them to pieces. The Idea will not disappear even if we all die, because it serves also those we are fighting. It is the same Idea for all of us, believed in by every one who holds a rifle. I know for a fact that we do not matter to it. It abandons us the moment we start killing one another, and flies back with the generals to Berlin or Moscow or London, and there seeks out new minds and new bodies, making people think that only it is their true, sacred mission and that they must let it into their hearts. It disappears as soon as it has seen them to the front, and everything starts all over again.

When I understood this, my days became dark and meaningless and I looked desperately for the meaning of why I am here in this place, because a man cannot live without meaning and if I believe anything it is only that. I worked out that the reason I am here must be something that came down with me into the trenches and helped me as I was digging out the dead after we had been shelled. I sought that thing day and night, and day and night I thought about you and missed you, until I saw that what I was looking for is you. You are my meaning. You are the reason I am here, the reason my rifle becomes hot and melts the snow, and then becomes so cold my skin sticks to it. That too is because of you. The reason is love, and it was for love I went to war. If I die, that too will be for love, and love will not die because it is eternal, only in a different way from all the words talked by the generals. Love takes pity, and it too does not care who wins in the end. I could never love you so much as I love you now if I had stayed at home. If it does not matter which country we have occupied or how many people we have killed, and I know for sure that it does not, and if it does not matter whether I am the killer or the one that someone kills, whether we conquer a country or it conquers us, then what does matter is the man himself and what is going on inside him. Right now, my darling, I am love itself, I am glowing with love for you. I can light a fire without matches and talk to God in the middle of a snowfield. I do not know who thought all this up or why, why everything has happened as it has, or why war is needed for love, but I have no doubt that everything depends on this, because nothing else was there with me in battle or will be there after I am dead. The Russky shooting at me madly, frantically loves his wife, and when I am shooting at him I am just as far in my thoughts and my soul from the battlefield. I am with you. I am hugging you and the children, and while our outward forms are killing each other, we are loving and the angels in heaven look down on us in admiration and give us praise. Now I have understood everything I am as happy as a child and I smile and am afraid of nothing, and I do not care whether we are advancing or retreating, whether we are encircled by the other side or have ourselves surrounded them. I do not care whether I am still alive or not, because that does not matter to our love, to which I swore my oath of allegiance.

Your husband, a soldier on the eastern front of love,

Günther Roth

VALERIA

It's funny, teenage Valya, but do you know when I was reminded of you again? About a week ago I went looking for a job, taking my time about doing the rounds of the city-centre cafes on Gutenbergplatz, which is long and into which the side streets from the railway station funnel like streams into a ditch, and the buses sail out like paper boats. It manages to fit in a red stone theater and wonderful old painted houses, meaningless concrete boxy department stores that look like Russian municipal buildings, a statue of Gutenberg wearing a hat, a glum clay pillar with a sign reading "Tree of Liberty" and a stunted fountain. I immediately ruled out all the cafes I used to frequent with Ralf, which considerably reduced the choice. Some places I did not like, some were not recruiting staff. I marched the length of the square to the point from which it flows, evidently a sculpted fountain looking like a streetlamp, because seven hundred meters in the opposite direction the square does quite clearly flow into the Rhine. You can always hear something plaintively splashing there and it is where my tram stops before, like a holiday resort donkey, climbing up a street like a ladder. A new cafe has been opened on the corner there, where the Schiller Cafe used to be. It's quite pleasant and even a little grand, and turned out to be a place where the Gas Queen, me, will be in her element. They took me on and, after some discussion, agreed I would work there three days a week.

Thank you, I accept your congratulations, only on my first day there, yesterday, I unhelpfully dropped a tray of glasses. Yes, sad butterfingers that I am, I tripped over the outstretched foot of a young man, fell sideways, and collapsed in a heap under the table of a party of girls. I placed the tray almost accurately in the midst of their shoes but, of course, the impact broke everything with an almighty crash. Then something unexpected happened. A German girl in a brown dress, you know the kind, with one of those long dreamy faces with full lips constantly parted, crawled under the table too and began helping me put the pieces on the tray. She was so anxious to help, she cut her fingers quite badly. I jumped up to get her a plaster, and a ginger-haired girl in their group caught me and whispered not to worry, they would say it had all been their fault. At this point the Chefin arrived with an expression of benign unconcern on her face. What an actress! If she wants to practice her acting skills the city theater is only a couple of hundred meters away. The redhead exclaimed, "We did it! It's all our fault! It was Christine." She pointed to the girl picking up the pieces. "She's taken up with a Russian and hasn't yet learned how to drink vodka, that's why she's being a bit wild." "How interesting," I thought. The girl under the table went quiet, uncertain whether or not to protest. The Chefin smiled primly and I rushed to the cupboard. I always carry plasters in my handbag.

When I got back I gave them to Christine (I made a point of remembering her name), and time seemed to stand still. You know how it is. I saw this still shot of me standing there with this German girl shifting around at my feet, as bloody and pitiable as a cat run over by a car. She quickly came out and went to the bathroom to rinse her minor wound. The only remaining evidence was the two plasters on her fingers. I cleaned everything up, apologized and thanked them, but that is not what matters. In that German girl under the table, I saw pimply, gawky you, Valya, unspeaking and willing, while everybody else is asleep, to quietly clean the whole world with your toothbrush. I suddenly realized you bore no grudge against those Germans who had been unkind to you: those adolescent girls who wore designer clothes (in whose eyes you in your Red Cross charity clothing were rubbish); for the whispered "Russian prostitute"; for the meanness, the betrayals, the complaints to teachers about the Russian upstart. I'm the one who's angry, who hates, who has had the meteoric career (Where are you now, girls from that school? My worst enemy's ambition was to be an interior decorator!), and I am two steps away from working for the most powerful company in the world, my dazzling take-off fuelled by hatred and the desire to really show those sad bitches. Yes, I am full of hatred and there is nothing I can do about it, but those were your eyes looking up at me from under the table, Valya, and it was to you I gave that plaster, to seal your lips and allow me to carry on being cold and successful.

While I was thanking the girls I took a good look at them. There were three: a tanned blonde with an indefinably telegenic face who had taken no part in the saga of the broken glasses (I think her name was Nina); then there was Silke, a gigantic curly redhead who rose, loud and energetic, above her blouse like a pudding (her spectacles really suited her, giving her some shape; without them she'd look like a shop assistant in a village store); finally, there was Christine, a small, not particularly striking but, on closer inspection, perfectly pretty little German girl. Redhead Silke asked me directly if I was from Russia. It wasn't too difficult to guess that from my accent. I cautiously answered affirmatively, joking, just in case, that unfortunately the cafe didn't stock red caviar. The next question might have been anything, from a request to sing "Dark Eyes" to abuse, but it was entirely straightforward. "McDonald's is holding an Asian Week, and we're having a Russian Day where I work," Redhead said. "Christine has met a Russian boy and is going on a date with him. We're giving her advice, so perhaps now we can ask you what to expect."

I was taken aback, immediately remembering my classmate Zhenia who had dropped her Ivan in favor of Sven, the most handsome German boy in the class. Their romance was over within a matter of days, even before I had time to be jealous, mainly because of the plotting of the German girls who spread dark rumors about Zhenia and set the class against her. She rejoined our Russian sector and we closed ranks. The ripples died down and equilibrium was restored, seemingly to the satisfaction of both sides. Then there was my affair with Ralf, which could hardly be classed a success, and now here was a Russian boy and a German girl. The only similar instances I could think of involved boys who were fully Germanized, whose only hint of Russianness was some exotic touch like a minor affectation of speech. What advice did I have to give? "If he wants to pay for you somewhere, don't object," I said, offering the only thing that came into my head. Redhead retorted: "And he will immediately assume he can use you as his own private property." But I was already running off to serve other customers.

The Chefin was keeping a close eye on me, so I had to keep running, which I wasn't used to and was soon tired and regretting having let nostalgia bring me back to working in a cafe. I discovered that while I was whirling around in a different world, a new generation of German girls had grown up, very attractive and more intent on having a good time than they were in my day. I am, after all, twenty-six already. What had become of those beanpoles with neither taste nor tact who strutted around like boys in their baggy Fila, Adidas and Nike sports gear? You couldn't risk dressing any other way or you'd be taken for a prostitute, or a sad throwback to whom nobody would give the time of day. Boys were still the same, there was no doubt about that, but girls had become more, well, Russian perhaps.

I got another order from the girls, four vodkas, a tomato juice and a pineapple juice. I brought it, and was unexpectedly offered the fourth vodka to drink to

"Mütterchen Russland", and to the hope that the incident with the tray was now safely behind me. It would have been churlish to refuse, so I took the glass as discreetly as I could, only to find that Silke was expecting me to propose a toast in Russian. With a glance towards the bar, I ceremoniously rattled off a stanza from Nekrasov's "Russian Women" which was still lodged in my memory from school. We clinked glasses, looked each other in the eye (a German tradition) and drained them. At the next table the boy whose leg I had tripped over wanted to pay his bill. He did not apologize, but left a five euro tip. I ran off briefly – after the vodka I seemed to be moving very smoothly, almost balletically – sorted out his bill, came back and freaked out. The blonde girl, who had been sitting so quiet and unremarkable, was explaining the poem to Silke and Christine, all about the sleigh wondrously wrought and the old Count, the heroine's father. I discovered that Nina, who most resembled those German girls who had derided me at school, had herself been born in Kazakhstan, but could not speak Russian now because she'd been brought to Germany while still a small child. "I can't speak it, but I understand almost everything," she confessed with a guilty smile. "Oh, and do you know, I so love Russian mushrooms. I go to the Russian store every week to buy them. But we only use Russian in our family for swearing."

Now I spotted a white T-shirt with a matryoshka doll under Nina's jacket. "Aha!" I thought. "That matryoshka is really hiding more than I thought." You know, Valya, I looked at her and, whether it was the vodka or all this sudden coming together of Russia and Germany, saw her as a little girl wrapped up from head to toe, carefully toddling along a path between snowdrifts. She was wearing so much clothing it was difficult to walk and suddenly, – plonk! – she slipped and fell in the snow. She was about to start crying when she realized there was no need because nothing was hurting. So instead she started laughing, a snowman's baby, a little cosmonaut in a spacesuit saying, "Hello, all you new people on the planet!" And at that very moment there would be a break of light blue sky and a fluffy cloud, which was about to climb in, a moment later would pull its foot back out and take itself off. Everything was such fun.

Best of all, though, I liked Christine. I smiled at her as I was running past with the trays, or perhaps I was smiling at you through her. I can't say it was all from the vodka. It's funny to recall the first time I tried vodka at Marina's. (She was my friend when I was seventeen or so.) We were sitting on the floor in the hallway, looking at imitation birch bark wallpaper which had been brought from Russia, and the corridor kept tilting to the right. There was juice flowing out of the birch trees, sweet rivers of birch juice, and they carried me away with them, and I slid over sideways and fell asleep.

MARK

You are not here. Any passerby, even if he is as empty as a balloon, can stop you by asking a stupid question, but for me you are not here. Any shop-window dummy can attract your attention; you are available for those who want to use your money or your body, for those who wish you ill, who find you ugly, but when my number is displayed, you do not answer the phone. You can be present in the life of beings whose very existence is open to question. It does not matter a jot whether they are in fact alive. To all intents and purposes they have no existence but yet they crowd around you, each trying to tear off a piece. That's how I see them, fleshless, stretching out toward you their trembling, sticky hands.

1, 2, 0, 0, 1, 0, 1. That is this past week. The number indicates how many times a day I called you. Sitting down with a piece of paper, I worked out which days of the week and what time of day would make my call to you look natural, a spontaneous act dictated not by any great need but by my passing mood. On Wednesday and Thursday I pretended to forget you, busy with my own concerns, only on Friday to suddenly remember and call to suggest (spontaneously) that we should meet up. You did not answer the phone. On Friday night and Saturday I pretended to be having a great time, and gave you a friendly call on Sunday, – sweetheart, how much further could I retreat? – to share our experience of the really cool weekend we had just spent apart. No dice. In formulating this plan I made a rough outline of what I would have been doing all week if I did not love you or loved you less. Some of it I actually did (not all that much, I suppose), some things I did mentally at the scheduled moment in order to be in the right frame of mind and not caught out if you did phone. For example, if under the plan a friend came round to talk shop, I would lie on my divan and talk to him in my mind. Okay, it sounds a bit silly, but it does help, because at times it looks like a rational plan for getting you back.

I'm already finding it difficult to tell what I've done in reality and what I only imagined. Events and days coalesce into a grisly mess. Wednesday and Thursday might seem to have been the worst because I didn't try to call you, but in fact on those days I felt a crescendo of excitement, like the band of an approaching parade, which peaked on Friday morning when my whole body was tingling and I had birds singing in my stomach. First, because I demonstrated to my own satisfaction my powers of forbearance; and second, because every hour I kept myself to myself improved the chances of the Friday call succeeding, or that you might phone me yourself. I was elated. I must have been radiant with happiness. The blue flame was spurting out of me like a fountain. I looked at the note detailing my busy life and worked with a will. Then, on Friday, when you again did not answer the phone, everything collapsed. I felt I had been strangled, and with the utmost difficulty persuaded myself back to persevere with the plan. By evening, however, my pecker was rising again and happiness flooded over me, deserting me only on Sunday when I made my last, futile, attempt.

Along with you, all colors and a considerable range of sounds have vanished. The world is blurred and I have difficulty making out objects. Everything I touch is rough and hard, and my fingertips seem slowly to be wearing away. I cringe at the thought of having to touch objects or myself. Things that once were smooth have grown a strange new skin. Sounds? Oh, yes, most of them have gone, but for some reason I still hear the tenderest, and there are even a few new ones. I never realized the world sounds so good. I notice it now every time I leave the apartment. Late one night, on the path near home, almost in the bushes, I heard the tinkling of Chinese wind chimes playing a wonderful tune. They moved away, drew closer, coming from somewhere above me, as if a pendulum were swinging. In the library as I was trying to read a book for a seminar, I was surrounded by the sound of splashing water. Who knows where that was coming from. You may laugh, but it was the sound of a stream in the forest, or perhaps it was just the plumbing. Then, of course, I have only to open the window when I'm home to hear the silky rustling of vehicles on Saarstrasse, as quiet as breathing, as gentle as having a damp sponge run over my skin. Perhaps, if I survive this whole episode, I may become a musician, but for now what good is all this beauty to me?

Today is Monday and I haven't drawn up a plan for this week. The scales seem to be weighed against me and time is not on my side. You're not beginning to miss me but just gradually forgetting me. I'm sitting at the window, staring blankly at that blurred world which consists entirely of lights, like the one crossing my window pane now. It's a plane taking off from Frankfurt Airport. Two hundred lives, compressed into a pinpoint between the upper and lower frames of my window. I feel I could catch it in my hand like a fly. Today I was nearly hit by a car. That might not have been such a bad thing: the physical pain would have been a distraction and I would have been taken to hospital. As it was, I just grazed my hands. I was crossing the road, probably against the red light, lost in my thoughts and your thoughts. A car came from around the corner, I jumped out of the way and fell on the road. I got away with a couple of bruises and some scratches on my hands. They were treated with antiseptic ointment. In the elevator I met a neighbor. She dragged me into her room, saying she knew what to do with wounds and is actually a nurse. While she was taking care of me, she kept saying what a pity it is that now in the hospital girls can no longer wear the surgical overalls because it disturbs the patients. Now they only wear a long jacket and white trousers.

I don't think I have anything to say to you. Last week I could have rattled off a whole novel but now I don't even believe in the possibility you might phone. No. You are not going to call and you are not going to come round. I have no further thoughts.

VALERIA

I was on my way to see my parents, squelching down the street to the tram. I found a seat by the window, and two stops later spotted Christine in a white BMW, next to a Russian boy (there was no two ways about it) I didn't know. The tram stopped at an intersection. I was staring absent-mindedly out the window when the car, like a faithful hound, itself crept up to where I was looking, meaning that I only had to try to remember where I'd seen this girl in her white jacket. She herself immediately remembered the incident at the cafe, squealed, poked her companion and pointed at me, saying something like, "Remember I told you I met a Russian waitress? That's her there!" He smiled and waved to me. He was tall and slim and, wearing an unseasonably sleeveless sports vest, evidently knew his own worth. I tried to mime through the glass an enquiry as to how her fingers were now. She understood, laughed and made a snipping movement with them to suggest she no longer had even a scratch. A moment later the car moved off.

Russian boys as strong as wolves, smashing their own and other people's heads and cars on any day of the week on lampposts and mirrors at Russian discos. I am not impressed. Only too often I've come across them in the offices of officials and training classes, timid and feeble, looking up through their eyebrows at fat, important Germans as if to say, "Please, mister, spare us a cent." How many times I've seen that transition from impotence to brute strength, when it seems the world is about to split on their backs like an undersized shirt. Their girlfriends, swarming around them like gnats, are Russian Germans, girls who have come here to work as nannies, or the Russian wives of local Germans. The boys drink vodka and light up like sparklers, only to stand dutifully the following morning in front of their German boss, and the next evening be back fizzing and punching faces and reaping admiring gazes from their Natashas and Marinas. The girls go on to qualify as nurses, accountants or sales assistants. It's not easy but girls always do what has to be done, while the boys are still wandering from one factory job to the next, and spending their money repairing cars they've smashed up while drunk. Then the family quarrels start, and she is pensive on her side of the bed while the boys are being enticed out of their family nests, lured by fresh, newly arrived Russian girls who are even younger and stupider and have longer legs and bluer eyes. Before long they too are pulling each other's hair in the toilets of discos, trying not to be dispossessed of their hero who is showing everyone his new toy car with a Kazakh or Russian flag stuck on its rear window.

For some reason I got off the tram in a really ratty mood, and in that state crossed the road, went into the station, and caught my train. German men struck me as no better than animals and Russian men as no better than pampered animals. Perhaps it was the patronizing smile that boy gave me, the obnoxious superiority he exuded. I should have got off the tram, smashed the headlights of his BMW, and shouted something like, "Who do you think you are? Have you any idea what I have achieved? Go sleep with your German girlfriend, but just don't look at me like that."

I closed my eyes and, in order to calm myself, imagined the train sledging downhill, sometimes bumping over hillocks which were towns, stopping to pant heavily through its open doors before speeding onward with the birds of the air over bare fields, clouds and orchards until I saw in front of me my parents' outwardly unprepossessing humpbacked house. It grew out of the bright room of my childhood, as if my father had brought seeds from Siberia, sown them, and on the good soil here the room had grown into a two-story house with a small basement.

In Russia we had a two-room apartment, but lived almost the whole time in one small room where it was winter all year round: all the furniture and the floor were covered in fluff from our knitting. The door to the other room was kept closed and we sat on a sofa in front of that door, behind which was a color TV set, a sideboard with crystal ware, a rug on the wall, many nice things, including something sparkling like diamonds, – and we knitted. Perhaps there was someone living in there, a completely different and happy family. For some reason it was very important for Father to feel he had a room where everything was civilized, a room which contained things that had been earned with sweat and blood, by honest German toil. It was his shrine, a place which, when times were at their most difficult, enabled him to hold on to his self-respect. There was no real need for us to go in there anyway.

It was Mother who started knitting goods for sale, at first in secret. She would knit when she was round with friends, and hid the finished sweaters and wool under my bed. My father was opposed to the "black market" trade and saw my mother's passion not as work but as a kind of fraud. He believed it was beneath the dignity of Germans. One day everything was discovered. I was awakened in the middle of the night and stood on the cold floor watching my enraged father pulling out wool and knitting needles and pieces of fabric from under my bed. There was a huge row but, thank God, I very soon went back to sleep. Then my father became ill and lost his job. The knitting needles gained legal status in our apartment, and selling sweaters became our sole source of income. Soon all three of us were knitting, mechanically, without looking at the knitting needles. We sat on the sofa in our wintry room watching a black and white TV and knitting sweaters in three colors: black, white and gray. We kept impeccably to the pattern. On the other side of the door a rainbow bloomed, the pages of books with orange and lemon spines rustled, the characters in our soap operas lived in a colored city, but we had no part in that life. When, just before moving to Germany, we sold that sofa, it retained three dents in its long seat, the imprint of our lives. What was behind the closed door had long been overgrown by weeds. Incidentally, our sweaters were of outstanding quality. The state-provided heating was not always reliable and warm clothes were much in demand. After a school celebration, I turned up to my first ever disco in a dress my mother had knitted. It was the same as the sweaters, only longer. I was in for a rude awakening. The girls were quite differently dressed, in light, tight-fitting, diaphanous dresses. There I stood in the doorway looking like the Snow Maiden emerging from the forest, wishing the ground would swallow me up. We had carefully brought our spinning wheels, knitting needles and wool, a lot of wool, with us to Germany. Somebody had told us knitting was a highly rated skill there. We found that knitted sweaters were readily available in any store and there was no market for ours, even cut-price.

I sometimes feel I'm still sitting knitting on that sofa, as if I just started day-dreaming one day and knitted together this whole world, this Germany where persimmons are seedless and where, if you post a letter, it will be in the hands of the addressee in the morning, so that not even the most militant addressee will have any grounds for demanding an explanation from the postman as to what has become of their letter. “Well, where is it? What have you done with my letter?” Under a woolen sky, woolen cars go by occupied by woolen Germans talking on their mobile phones about money. In Siberia we never had enough money, which is why in this woolen country everybody is so obsessed with it, and somehow we no longer get round to writing poetry. I was not very skillful, I’m afraid, and was only too happy if I managed to sell something I’d knitted in some chilly city.

At one of the stations, about fifteen minutes from home, an elderly gentleman in a blue shirt sat next to me. I opened my eyes for a moment, then closed them again and was back on the sofa, where it was as if we were spinning a spider’s web to catch the people who lived in the bright room next door. Before long I had to open them again because someone was complaining loudly. We’d been stationary for about five minutes in the middle of a field. I took out my mobile and warned my father I would be a bit late, as he was meeting me at the station.

“Where are you from?” the man in the shirt enquired oversolicitously.

“Russia.”

He demanded clarification, observed that it was cold in Siberia, and told me that actually he was a specialist in refrigeration. “We manufacture something that is free in Siberia!” Without any transition, he started telling me how lonely he was. We must have clogged the train wheels with wool. Sweaters were piled high on the rails preventing our onward progress. We were stuck here and this old German geezer was gradually earthing me up like a row of potatoes, leaving me to decide whether it was worth my time to go off with him, eat, drink, and spend a little of his money, admire something about him, let him clutch me briefly and give himself a bit of a shake. There was nothing in what he was saying that could be construed as offensive, but what he was getting at with all this beating about the bush, all this cowardly, risk-free chatting up (and he did make it abundantly clear what he was after and how much he was willing to shell out) suddenly nauseated me. I made my excuses, squeezed past his knees and walked to the end of the car. I stood at the window, watching everything outside passing in layers: a field, houses, the ribbon of the Rhine, the vineyards on the slopes, and even a forest sprinkled on the very top. I live in a botanical garden where the scenery changes like the suits in a game of cards. Everything has lost its primal value. Nature herself has lost her edge and been domesticated, and they even want to put a leash on girls from Siberia.

He came along to the vestibule, said nothing, but sat on a hinged seat and sighed meaningfully a few times. It was all so dumb I was beginning to find it amusing. Why do I get upset by men, Russian or German? The whole lot of them are just little kids, all hoping this is going to be their lucky day. It's just that in Germany that means getting what you want on the cheap. Isn't that right, shirt man? Anyway, that sad old person who took me to court doubtless thought he was standing up for the old, traditional order, except that not even the country I was carrying beer in ten years ago still exists. He needs to take a look at today's German girls in a cafe. His is a world of false memories and crazy ideas about the world which are actually rather sweet. As for that Russian boy, I guess he didn't do anything all that bad, just smiled and waved. So what if we understood each other instantly, and he was preening himself like a rooster on a fence. In a BMW with a pretty German girl beside him, who wouldn't feel like top baboon in the troupe? I smiled, the train started, strode through two stops in next to no time and, at a station which looks like a cuckoo clock, on a platform where the very best German in the world, my dad, was waiting for me, I disembarked.

MARK

Once upon a time there was a girl who loved to lie in men's arms. She had only to close her eyes for the bed to seem like a raft sailing across a lake. She was the tsarina of the raft, and only her laws applied on it. Anyone who did not obey her was beheaded. She also loved recalling her exes and nothing in this world, not eclipses of the sun nor storms nor pirates' attacks, could stop her talking about them. It used to seem as if they were swimming alongside the raft, unconvincingly pretending to be water lilies. Even more than remembering her exes, though, she liked to be warm, so three blankets were constantly on duty on the raft and she had the phone number of the god in charge of the weather and would periodically ask him for a miracle to add a degree or two to the climate over the lake. This tsarina had grown up without anyone else influencing her, so her tastes were really very basic, not at all refined. Reclining on her royal cushions, she would munch potato chips washed down with water from the lake, and watch movies pirated from the Internet, which was how she learned about new things going on outside her world. And her world consisted of three elephants bearing a chalice on their trunks which contained the lake. They were standing on the broad shell of a turtle which, oddly enough, was swimming in the very lake the elephants were holding up, so that neither the court astronomers nor the court astrologers could give any halfway sensible explanation of what was holding up what and how. That did not perturb the tsarina in the slightest, and she especially did not give a toss about all that kind of stuff when she was lying in someone's arms and telling them about her exes. If the tsarina announced she wanted to sleep, then within two or three minutes she would be snoring like a pig, thereby demonstrating how splendidly she kept her royal word. If as she was sleeping anyone were tentatively to touch her, she would frown with displeasure and turn over on to the other side. There was also a game she played in the night. She would wake up and cover all the parts of her royal body which had escaped from the duvet like animals from a zoo, and also cover up the person who a short while before had been holding her in his arms, in order to be able to tell him proudly in the morning that she had done so. Friends, I too used to sail on that raft, but one time I must have incurred her royal anger. I was thrown into the water and demoted to the status of a water lily. For a long time I trailed in her wake, trying with my petals to catch hold of the edge of the raft and clamber back on. One time I almost succeeded, but someone as they passed dislodged me with their toe. I fell back into the water and, from shame and chagrin, drowned.

Italian, Dutch, French, Spanish, Turkish, Arabic, American, Brazilian? I really don't know, so don't torment me. Australian Eskimo? Why not? Austrian, Hungarian, Polish, Czech, Swedish, Danish, Finnish? Russian? I'm sitting in Nina's room trying to guess the nationality of your new boyfriend. Yes, the one you're perhaps right now making love to. It's Nina's stupid idea. After every word I utter, the light is turned on for an instant in your bedroom and I see you naked, clutching blond Scandinavians, or Spaniards with a tattoo on their shoulder, or God only knows who else. Sometimes the images are superimposed and then you're in bed with two men, a black African, say, and a white skinhead, and they have casually thrown their arms over your body and this has caused peace to break out between them.

Looking at this picture gallery would be unbearable if this were the first time I was doing it. Alas, baby, the first time it is not. A Russian, then. The light goes back on in the bedroom, but lying with you I see only an unclear figure, someone in a long military greatcoat. Stop! Nina, don't tell me you acted as go-between!

No, she had no part in it. Nina is Russian, although, if she did not tell you as much you might not guess. She has grown up in Germany. So where did you find him, my darling? I allow the light to shine mercilessly in the bedroom one more time, and a bearded, bear-like man is pawing you. He immediately blows up and bursts like a balloon. The Russians are a strange lot. Just as, in the nineteenth century, they were divided into a handful of dashing men in uniform, the heroes of Tolstoy's novels, and a mob of bearded peasants, so now out of the torrent of threatening, ugly characters I encounter in the street in their tracksuit pants and leather jackets, like a jack-in-the-box someone as gorgeous as tennis star Marat Safin can pop up and carry you away from me.

Nina is making me a cup of tea. I sit in her kitchen and look at the jars on the shelves. The labels are in Russian, with illustrations which most probably depict something edible, but which I cannot identify, something round, smiley, indeterminate. I wonder how similar this kitchen is to that of your Russian, who probably also eats these things and will treat you to them, and you'll be sure to ask him what the dish is called in his language, and will be sure to pronounce it in a funny way, after which you'll both burst out laughing and then start kissing.

Nina is busy, standing with her back to me, washing

cups. The Russian jars on the shelves say in her voice, "Mark, I decided to invite you here to tell you about Christine's new boyfriend, not because I want to hurt you," (You've managed that anyhow, jars) "or dot all the 'i's between you." (Is there anything still in need of clarification?) "Not at all. I wanted to have this conversation with you (blah, blah, blah) for one reason only, and because you and Christine are no longer together. That is, you have ceased to be a part of her life." (Do just shut up!) "Hence for me and her other friends your role is no longer that of someone with whom we socialize because of our friendship with Christine, and instead you gain value as just yourself, as a friend and a nice person. What it comes down to is that you're breaking up only with Christine, and there is no reason for us, her friends, to delete you from our lives. I can't deny that these past eighteen months you were a beautiful couple, but just on your own you really look quite dishy, and though for now you are not on speaking terms with her, times change, wounds heal. I'm talking primarily about your own wound, Mark, because Christine has taken it all very stoically, and you'll go back to being old friends, only on a higher level, because jealousy and resentment will fade and only shared pleasant memories will remain, and the understanding that comes when a man and a woman have gone to sleep and woken up in the same bed."

Somewhere in the middle of her speech, I switched off. How stupid I am. All along I could sense you had someone else, but until this conversation had no idea that, like a man flying in the sky by holding on to a clutch of balloons, I was clinging to the stupid, childish fantasy that, at least for the present, you would not start relationships with other men. I fell, my feet going straight through clouds glued carelessly together out of gift wrapping paper with pictures of sad-eyed teddy bears. Then I was in an enormous elevator but it made little difference. The elevator too was falling, only I was not alone in it. Next to me were naked men whose skin was of every color, all those I had seen in your bedroom, and they too were sad-eyed, and they were all turned to face me. The African and the skinhead were still holding hands, and someone put a sympathetic hand on my shoulder. One of us, the Indian, I think (you told me once he took you to a restaurant), the only man wearing swimming trunks (which had a picture of a monkey eating a banana on them), pressed the emergency button to call for help. After a while the speaker crackled, there was a rustling noise and a cheerful voice drawled, "Today, and only today, we have some very special guests. It is your very good fortune to have a folk music quartet from Leningrad to play for you. Stay tuned to this channel." An unknown person cleared his throat and blasted the elevator with a loud, powerful "KA-A-A-A" – there was a moment's pause before – "LINKA, Kalinka, Kalinka, my love, TA-TA-TA-TA-TA Kalinka, Kalinka, my love." "Why don't you dance?" The Indian asked. The (female) monkey on his trunks gave me a wink and started eagerly peeling the banana. I looked around. The naked men were dancing with their arms round each other's shoulders. The African and the skinhead appeared to be dancing a tango. "Why did you never dance with her? You know how much she wanted that. Do you understand now that you could not give her all she needed to be happy? It was in a disco that she met Andrey." I opened my eyes. I was sitting in a chair and all around stretched burning sands of linoleum so yellow they hurt my eyes. The wallpaper too was yellow and the desert extended as far as the eye could see. I was desperately thirsty. A mirage appeared on the horizon. I got up and staggered towards it. From above, a biblical voice was intoning that a certain Christine, too, had not been wholly in the right, that some things should be done differently, and that there are times when you really ought not to lose your head. When I was too tired to stagger on any further, I found the mirage right under my hands: it was Nina's vest. The jars were silent, their foolish round faces staring anxiously down at me. Nina froze into immobility, before carefully moving the cups to one side and pressing her hands down on the kitchen table. Somewhere below there was a skirt. I raised it like a curtain and started undoing my belt, but before that justice had to be done and I swept the Russian jars above me off their shelf. Two, I think, smashed and one with a rumbling sound rolled out of the kitchen to bemoan its fate to the toilet door. It was followed by my belt and all the rest.

VALERIA

"Bunnies, are you bored? Why don't I come and sit beside you?" A young man, who had been irresolutely hanging around the far end of the yard, came over to us. He was speaking Russian. Christine looked at me anxiously, as if seeking protection, and I immediately felt like the Amazon with a long sword I dreamed of being when I was little, or perhaps just a guard dog protecting our yard. This is my territory, the benches under the poplar trees and the ping-pong table heaped with leaves. My windows look out on this poplar bastion, and if I'm flying in my dreams I doubtless find my way back to them by sound, the familiar whispering of the trees and the theme tunes of the programs on Russian Channel One which emanate from every second window.

"No, we're not bored, so please don't pester us." I was neither upset nor angry, but I felt like bawling someone out, and it came two degrees ruder than I intended. He stood around for decency's sake for another twenty seconds before disappearing into the next but one entrance along, where he lived. I had seen him in the courtyard several times before. He had been looking at us from his window, and he was not the only one. The ever-watchful grannies who had just finished viewing Russian channels on satellite TV were also peering at us quizzically from their windows, because we were covered with a lid in the form of a dark sky in which, judging by the lack of stars, there were invisible goings-on going on. Something was busy scratching as every one of us was stewing in the same pot and we all needed to know everything about each other, just as the carrot in the stew knows everything about the onion. Thus, right now an old granny in a knitted beret with an ornamental band on it is observing us from the balcony over the third entrance. She has her hands hidden in a box, as if she is molding a model of us from life at the same time as quarreling with an invisible woman in the room. We can hear, "All right, all right. Why don't you..." From the side where I live comes the sound of music, the feline voice of a woman is singing Russian lyrics, although from our bench all you can hear are the rhymes – stream-dream, newborn-dawn. It's more than enough.

"You say Russians have not forgotten how to love, Russians have monopolized love, but I'm the one in love and you're not. Christine's big, moist, newborn-dawn eyes gaze at me. They are serious, almost black. Night has filled them with pools of water. I cannot think of an answer. I don't know what to say to you, my younger self.

Christine turned up in the cafe half an hour before closing time, trembling and frightened. She said she urgently needed to speak to me, then waited inaudibly in the corner as long as necessary. We went outside together and my tram, the last to my district this evening, immediately approached. Fine, let's go to my place! As we drove along I was watching the leg of a girl sleeping in her Turkish mother's arms slowly slipping down into a bag of groceries. Christine quietly explained her problem to me. A Russian girl had come up to her in the street today and threatened in broken German that if she did not leave Andrey alone she would be very sorry indeed.

"I mean, I've never even seen her before, and she stared at me as if I were her worst enemy, as if I were a criminal, like I had murdered her baby or something. As if I were the cause of all her troubles, when I'm just going about my business, not interfering with anyone, and just want to be nice. She hates me, but what for? How can she behave like that? What kind of people are you all? What century are you living in? Every last one of you has a German passport. There are civilized ways of dealing with this sort of situation. I am perfectly happy to talk to her and listen to her point of view."

I listened to Christine as we were riding along and as we walked along the pathway, and with every stride the poplars in my courtyard grew another degree taller. "Hello, Aunt Zina. Where are you off to so late?" Aunt Zina rolled past us like a big pink ball and it occurred to me that Christine had been taken prisoner, like the Germans at Stalingrad, and perhaps she too was now at the mercy of the conqueror. Or perhaps she was caught in the crossfire. She had got involved in a game whose rules she did not know.

"Of course you have murdered her baby. Do you think she hadn't already chosen his name? Alyosha, probably."

"What?"

"Al-yo-sha. Of course, this baby was only born in her head after they had split up, if there even was anything serious. Perhaps they just happened to sleep together after some disco."

Oh, I know the way they pull these babies out of their hats at just the right moment. They get used as bargaining chips. A dozen such offspring may be killed off just to get back at an ex-boyfriend. They push them in his face, they gamble with them. They are the most reliable currency, unborn babies. And born babies too.

"Valeria, d'you think you might have some vodka at home? Right now I feel like a drink."

So now we're going in the opposite direction, back toward the tram stop, and Aunt Zina in her pink jacket is crawling ahead like a ladybug. It's not far to the gas station where there's a round-the-clock store familiar to all our yard's residents. And I keep banging on:

"You don't know what she cooked specially for him, or what she let him get up to in bed. Perhaps she'd never let anyone before him do that sort of thing, yet he dumped her all the same, and then you turn up, beautiful, successful, and German. Who's she going to take it out on? She idolizes him, so that leaves you. She doesn't think she can get him back this way, but for the moment she's like a wounded she-wolf. Of course, if you decide to stay with him, you've got it made. He'll be able to protect you. Men like that."

"He's an ex-soldier."

"From the Bundeswehr?"

"No, he said he was in the Army when he lived in Russia."

"Well there you are!"

Except that I understand nothing. What's the connection? What has brought together this oddity with his dubious past, obviously a womanizer and most probably caught up in shady dealings with a stack of women who almost certainly have children, either here or back in Kazakhstan, and a German girl who is little more than a child herself and completely alien to this world? It's not as if anybody is forcing her, and yet for some reason she's holding out for this Russian of hers with whom she says she is in love. She has come running to me, instead of just instantly sending him packing. How has she had time to fall in love with him?

In the alcohol section of the shop two Russian boys of about fifteen were staring slack-jawed at the shelves. We materialized like two alcoholic fairies and, in some embarrassment, I pulled out what we were after. Having spent next to no time there, we vanished. I stashed away the bottle, some plastic cups and a pack of juice in a bag and, for the fourth time that evening, thought how much I hated the ringtone on her phone which, yet again, Christine was not answering. Once more, now excited, we hastily retraced out steps to the courtyard. A lone taxi drove past, the leaves rolling like apples from under its wheels over the asphalt.

We decided to stay outside and settled ourselves on the bench. Perhaps Christine wanted to maintain the appearance of a business meeting, after which she would be able to make a considered decision. Except that it is a long time since our Russian courtyard was neutral territory.

"You see, Andrey is brave and strong, but before I met him I never felt I needed protection. What he might protect me from only appeared after he became part of my life. It came along with him." Christine spoke slowly, choosing her words carefully. People used to speak to me like that when my German was still sketchy. "It was he who brought danger into my life, and you Russians are the cause of it, with your insane Russian way of life with which you infect everything, even this courtyard. The danger came with you, and the remedy for it also comes from you, even if it's only in this bottle. Why did I just now want to drink with you, and why particularly vodka? With you it's as if I'm no longer myself."

I poured a little vodka into the plastic cups. We drank almost without interest, without clinking glasses, and as always the world with its billions of miles of space, upwards with its hovering angels and airplanes, downwards with its moles, bones, and the earth's blazing core, which I sensed with all my organs of perception, even my skin, shriveled and shrank from the alcohol to the size of our courtyard, and even smaller, to the size of the wooden bench on which we sailed, describing slow circles round the poplar trees, as if we were on the rim of a revolving gramophone record.

Christine went on grumbling that we wanted to infect her too and draw her into our senseless, merciless world, but I was no longer feeling anything other than love for this little space squeezed in between the apartments and cut off from the rest of the senseless world, like a closed desk drawer. But the rest of the world was neither forgotten nor abandoned. Pipelines ran beneath it along which from somewhere in the east, cubic meter by cubic meter, came love, and I was ready to take my place in the ranks and work and build and do everything to light up Germany too with this steady blue glow. We drank some more, and I tried as best I could to tell her about my wish and the new place where I'd be working, and about love, but she took umbrage and said her ex-boyfriend had talked like that, except that from me it seemed less boring. Then someone wanted to join us and we shooed him away. We drank some more and Christine, who a couple of minutes earlier had been trembling with fear, suddenly flew into a rage which, given how puny she is, looked quite funny.

"Who does she think she is? What an opinion she's got of herself! Thinks she can walk up to me like that and I'll be so scared I'll let her have my boyfriend? I'll show her where she gets off. Come on, Valeria, let's find her and give her a good thrashing! Or perhaps she's here. Russians live here, don't they? Well, where are you? Come on out!" The last words she yelled up into the dark windows. Any Russian grannies who were not already standing behind their curtains, now took up position, only they didn't yet have the courage to put Germans in their place, so their windows remained silent.

I took Christine to my apartment. If I remember, on the way up the stairs I was assuring her she had nothing to fear and that Andrey and I would protect her and she'd never see that girl again. Russians were great people, only who wouldn't get upset if someone made off with their boyfriend?

"Yes, Russians are great!" she bawled into the stairwell. "Russians are great!"

When we got in, we turned on the TV. I had the Russian channels, on one of which a woman with no waistline was throatily singing a song about the Volga. She was small and squat but her voice so elevated her that she rose up on tiptoe, and then it escaped from her as if from a tight little closet, rose upwards to the ceiling and there exploded like the fireworks at New Year and settled like dust on the shoulders of the audience.

Andrey had taught her how to tie a headscarf the Russian way, like the Russian grannies. She promptly found a suitable cloth and tied it around her head, which made her look older and very Russian and loveable. Seating herself on the sofa, she began comically giving herself airs, said she was a tsarina, and commanded that more vodka should be brought. I hugged her and told her she was not a tsarina but my little squirrel sister from a fairy tale, and all men could go to hell.

MARK

A strong wind was blowing. The treetops were beating their heads against each other the way noses bump together when you kiss. On the way from the tram stop to my home I only once met passersby: a boy was carrying a girl on his shoulders, the way people carry little children. They smiled and expected me to smile back but I couldn't, and their look of bewilderment was left behind on the path, as if they feared I might run at them and topple their house of cards. I pulled out my notebook and wrote, "Lord, send me someone to hate, someone to blame that she's not with me. Let me live empty, pointless, useless years without her without being tormented every day, every hour and every minute. Take away my brain so that I can find solace in a foolish phrase which explains everything; let me become obsessed with some crazy notion; let me sprout thorns; let me foam at the mouth with rage. Loving is unbearable. I ask of you only that you lighten my burden. Mark." I tore the page out, folded it in half, and woke the yellow mailbox with a snap of its metal door.

Baby, you of all people must know that what I have done was just a pathetic parody of revenge. That was not me fucking Nina, it was my despair fucking my impotence. You shot me at point blank range without even taking aim, without even half-closing your sweet eye, not deigning even to give me that. You walked away but I came scurrying after you, huffing and puffing, ran up to you with my wooden popgun, puffed out my cheeks and made the sound of a shot with my lips. You didn't even turn round. When you left, you forgot me; you didn't notice my revenge, but out of the sky like in a computer game, a sign appeared which said, "Mission Accomplished. You are quits. You have taken revenge. 10 points." A dead man is supposed to lie down. It's a sign of nobility of spirit, of humility. People respect him for it, but a corpse which won't stop counting, a cadaver which carries on gaming, is absurd and pathetic. I sold the beauty of my love to the first dealer I met for a couple of cents and made it sordid, petty and vindictive. Knowing that I will never fall in love with anyone again. I failed my very first test and swallowed the hook of surrogate revenge like a stupid fish. A Russian fucked my girl so I needed to fuck a Russian girl. What wonderful logic. Applause! The audience chokes on its own rapturous ovation! What a hero! Zorro Mark II! Will you forgive me this travesty, Christine, as I forgive you for being able to live without me?

The house would not let me in. The key fought furiously in the keyhole but I couldn't turn it. I had to walk round the building to the second entrance. After taking only a few steps, I slipped on some muck in a plastic bag, hurt my knee and fell to the ground. Sitting there, I was the size of a four-year-old; lying down I was the size of a hedgehog, a rabbit or a small cat, and when I shut my eyes I was just an empty black spot. Sprouting up like grass growing through asphalt, the cold rose into me. The soil smelled of earthworms. Lord, I have no strength left. I no longer want to breathe or eat or

see

anyone

ever again...............

From the void I came and to the void I shall return.

The moment I stepped out of the elevator, my neighbor peeped out of her door, the one who salved my cuts and bruises after I was nearly run over. Cocking her head to one side, she watched me fumbling with my keys.

"Well, what was it this time?"

"I slipped."

"Wait right there. I'll just get some ointment and a bandage."

"No, don't. I won't open the door to you."

"As you will. In that case I shan't come over."

But she did, and I did.

The next morning I walked into the office of the newspaper for which I write about youth issues. You will doubtless appreciate that any issues young people are going to face today will be solely because I find it unendurable to stay at home in my thirteenth circle of hell. Christine, you are arranged in every corner of my apartment. I placed you everywhere, the way people position a tall vase of dried bull-rushes in a corner. You have a special corner where you pretend to be a whore and slip down the shoulder straps of your shift. Yesterday, after what I'd done, there was moaning coming from that corner all night as you fucked your Russian. All night. Can you imagine it?

I was still limping, and had turned up to work in jeans still muddy from yesterday's fall. I told a colleague, a lovely woman who had moved from East Germany who began quizzing me about my appearance, that I had spent the night on a mission for the Party. She nodded and left the nutcase in peace. I sat down at a free computer and looked out the window. An oriental girl was walking briskly down the street with her head held high while a balding Arab carrying bags tried to keep up. He was constantly shouting after her, pleading. Now and again she would look round to make sure he was following, and if he fell too far behind she would slow down a little. I think I felt hatred for her, but had no time to fully savor the feeling because I was called in to see the boss.

The boss looked silently at my jeans for some time.

"Are you a young journalist?"

"Excuse me?"

"Are you a young journalist?"

"Yes." I could not see where this was leading.

"Florian Kumpf has been admitted to hospital. Can you stand in for him at a conference for young journalists?"

"Yes, of course!"

The blue corner, the green corner, the red corner, the yellow corner... Yesterday I slipped and fell because I had been tossed like a coin and came down tails, which meant I will steer clear of all these Russians fucking Christine, fucking me, fucking this country, fucking, fucking, fucking.

"Do you know where it is being held?"

"No, it doesn't matter."

"Why are you looking such a mess? You haven't been over-generous lately with your visits to us. You have allowed yourself simply not to carry out your last two assignments, without explanation."

"I know. I apologize. It won't happen again. I was ill and worried about my exams. I want to go on this assignment. I have a lot of ideas about youth journalism."

Herr Schenke, let me go! This is my opportunity. I need to get right away from here, to contract into a dot between the frames of my window and land in a different city, preferably a different country. I will lose myself among the passersby, leave myself in the main square like a torn shirt, and when I come back I'll try to start everything from scratch again.

"Very well, as you are so keen. Incidentally, your present appearance will be entirely appropriate to where you're going. The conference is being held in Russia, in a city called Voronezh."

"No. I won't go."

"Aha, changed your mind already. Think about it. It's being organized by a major gas company. Caviar, champagne, pretty girls. Even snow. Naturally, we shall expect an article from you about the conference and your general impressions."

I feel I'm being constantly beaten on the same spot, beaten mercilessly with no time to recover my senses and without being able to see the fist or the stick doing the beating. Someone is taking my nightmares and trying to turn them into reality, within a budget which has been allocated for the purpose. Evidently no expense is now being spared: my "sponsor" is an all-powerful oil company. Voroshshsh, Voronshsh… As if the whole thing was the fault of that Russian, as if all was not already lost even before you met him, as if you were not sending someone a text message that night when you tucked your legs into a tube of folded blanket, when I woke up because a page had been turned in my dream. As if I had not heard you say, "Let's not talk about it. I can't tell you anything at the moment. I don't know what I feel. Mark, sometimes I feel your love is crushing me like a heavy wall, suffocating me. Give me room to breathe, Mark."

"Can I think about it?"

"Unfortunately not. I need your passport on my desk before four o'clock today. I have to send the forms to the consulate at four. If there was more time we would find someone to send to the conference in whom, right now, we had more confidence. Do I make myself clear? This is an opportunity for you and, I'm afraid, also your last chance."

"Fine. I'll go and get my documents."

"Excellent. I'll look forward to seeing your article. I hope the FSB doesn't give you any polonium tea. Ha-ha."

Don't expect me to react, Herr Schenke. I'm way past laughing. If I was offered polonium tea I would drink it.

"I'm joking, of course. I'll expect an honest, objective, professional report, like those you so pleased us with when we first started working together."

"Could you repeat the name of the town?"

"Of course, just a moment." He looks at the name on the paper on his desk. "Vo-ro-nezh."

"Where is it?"

"Google, Mark. Google has been invented."

I was rummaging through various boxes looking for my passport when the phone rang. It was Nina. Goodbye, Nina, goodbye, so long. I'm emigrating to Russia to live on the shores of a lake on which I'll launch boats with sails made of birch bark, silent, powerless, frail, circling on black Russian water like balletic swans until one day they shake off their feathers and fly away, and I'll follow them with my eyes until they vanish behind the mountains, or hills, or fells or whatever the Russians have not yet demolished to get iron and coal.

"I can't. I'm flying out to a conference. It's work. No, it's got nothing to do with you or Christine. Just work. Nothing to do with Andrey either. By the way, who is he?"

I can explain who he is much better, baby. He's the man who, when no one can see you, puts his hand on your ass, and you arch your back in a feline female reflex.

VALERIA

I woke up at around three in the morning thinking I was running out of boards, which meant I could not finish building something. I listened for a few minutes to the quiet ticking of the room and wondered what my building jag was all about. Then I remembered. I was building a flying ship in my dreams again.

Immediately, school came back to me, the spring, break-time, and I'm dragging into the bushes a cold, wet, once green board with peeling paint and nails sticking out of it. Where it lay the grass is white and worms are entwined with the roots of plants. The boards had already turned into the earth's skin, but they were the best I could find. I pulled out of the ground all there were within a radius of several hundred meters of the school, missing out only a place where some boys once hanged a cat. I piled all my materials in a secret hiding place. Yes, they were rotten, yes they were rubbish, but what do you think you build a flying ship out of, and if I didn't build it, how come I'm here?

It tugged and pulled at its tether, and the rope holding it was as taut as a guitar string. From up there the school yard looked like just a square shape; the clouds were its ocean and the birds leaped like dolphins. We flew out at night. Down below the lights of the towns were blurred by our speed, like comets. We humans and animals, our family plus the rabbits, the cow and her calf, the pigs, chickens, cats, dogs and frogs, were flying through the night standing on the deck. We Snow Germans came to Russia on a ship and so, naturally, it was on a ship we were leaving.

The first thing was photos from relatives who had gone to Germany started turning up in the hands of our friends. They were very strange snapshots. In comparison with our part of the world there was a clear over-abundance of vegetation. The photographs seemed to glow in the dark like fireflies. People whom we remembered as no different from ourselves were transfigured. They looked younger, they were well dressed, in the midst of idyllic landscapes filled to bursting with rose bushes, massive treetops, lakes with swans, castles, views from hills, and even some unbelievable amusement parks. I do not remember seeing any photos taken inside a house. There was only the outdoors, as if now they were living in the Garden of Eden. It would have been interesting to know what these people from another world ate, how their apartments were laid out, but they did not tell us that and we had to draw our own conclusions from hints casually dropped. One former neighbor wrote that her children were so spoiled they might start eating a Mars chocolate bar only to leave half of it on the windowsill. I used to be paid a Mars bar for every sweater I had knitted that was sold, so I knew their value and could only conclude that the children must be very stupid.

First you got "the number" (I never really knew the proper name of this document). Then came the invitation and you could leave. I think obtaining the number was the difficult part, after which the invitation was fairly automatic and you only had to wait for it. Grandmother's eldest sister, Aunt Lise, moved to Germany back in the 1970s through the Baltic states. In their youth she and grandmother had fallen out and for more than twenty years there had been no contact between them, but now that Lise was inviting the whole family back to Germany, to the green pastures of heaven, a grand reconciliation was anticipated.

I adored my grandparents. Grandpa would sit on a stool smoking a pipe and, through two doorways, would watch the news from the hallway on a television which stood in the bedroom. He would have backed even further away but that was the extent of their house. It was built of mud and straw and was, to all intents and purposes, a dugout. Grandma Else would walk past, waving the smoke away and muttering, "Pfui Teifel". She herself only watched soap operas. They had a box full of baby chicks in their house and, when there was no one around, I would plunge my hands in and pull the warm, yellow balls of fluff out and rub my face in them, as if I were washing in chicks. They would peck comically at my nose.

Every year I spent my summer vacations with my grandparents in northern Kazakhstan. An incredible number of creatures lived there in a very small area. There were even frogs living in the shower. They all seemed to be eating each other and to be perfectly happy. I was a similarly small creature, much smaller than the pigs, Chernushka the Cow, or Seryi the Dog, who was kept on a chain. I was in the same league as the chickens and rabbits but enjoyed certain privileges. There was no probability of my being eaten. The innocent creatures around me would die in the most bizarre manner. Headless roosters ran around the yard, rabbits' skins were crucified on special frames, Colorado beetles were drowned in diesel fuel, kittens in ordinary water. Pigs were castrated without any attention paid to their all-to-human screams. Each year, however, brought a cycle of renewal. Every chicken knew it would be taken and that a successor would come in its stead. All the animals seemed to feel gratitude and devotion to their owners up to the moment of their death. I was the first to leave this setting, and a year later Grandma and Grandpa themselves left for Germany.

Their house was emptied. Apart from the frogs, all the animals were killed. Only the cats and dogs were partly given away or set free to fend for themselves. Chernushka, Grandma's favorite, was taken away to the meat factory. It was a terrible blow. Of all the great, splendid cows in the village, she was the smallest and slenderest and yet gave no less milk than the others. In any case, milk yields were nothing to do with it. A whole world came to an end for no reason, just like that, but I knew that every one of the animals, even the very smallest, really only migrated to the flying ship and was looking down on us, earnest and puzzled.

By the time my grandparents arrived, we were already living in the western part of Germany. My parents were proud of how quickly they managed to find a highly suitable apartment for the old people. It was tidy and light and had an echo, two rooms in a ten-story inner-city block. They came, took a look at me, a wild child with luxuriant acne, and hugged me as if we had never met before. They got furniture from the neighbors, and from us they got a television someone had thrown out and Dad repaired. Timid and pitiable, they came out for a walk with us. Like a television presenter, my mother rapturously announced the next of the city's sights. I tagged along silently through the avenues of the municipal parks, just as superfluous and out of place here as the old folk. You could have credibly sent the three of us out to beg.

My parents were enjoying life. They both had jobs and had established friendly relations with their colleagues. Back home, the old folk watched television, talk shows in which, in a barely comprehensible language, half-naked girls discussed oral sex and whether they should lose weight or were fine as they were. They always decided they were fine as they were. In the mornings my grandparents would go with a little shopping bag on wheels to the supermarket, but never bought much. My grandmother refused to cook produce she was not familiar with. The household chores occupied no more than one hour a day and with the best will in the world they couldn't think of anything more to do. The apartment was empty and derisively spotless. Their life was over.

Finally, the great day of reconciliation arrived. Aunt Lise came from Hamburg. She was a dried-out old German woman who had all but forgotten Russian. Her fluffy white head with its big red mouth was almost hidden by dark glasses. Grandma hugged her first and started to cry, a big, fat elderly lady in a white headscarf and a misshapen woolen sweater. She looked like an old hen trying to foster a brood of rubber ducks. Aunt Lise immediately adopted a comforting, joshing tone, flashing her dazzlingly white new teeth, and made no attempt to conceal her disdain for us. She appeared to have written me off as a symptom of the family's degeneracy. The sisters had nothing to say to each other. Their lives had turned out very differently. My grandma had spent her entire life in the same village without ever learning to read or write. She went to school for the first time only after the collapse of the USSR, but by then it was too late and there were no good teachers left. Lise had her first years of primary education when they were still in the Ukraine, in a school with a portrait of the Führer on the wall. She was taught to read and write German, and then learned Russian from Yefim. As soon as the ethnic restrictions were lifted, she went to study in the town. She married, divorced, quarreled with the entire family and settled in Latvia, where she spent almost ten years trying to move to Germany, for which she was terribly homesick despite never having been there.

Grandma looked not just Russian, but impossibly

Russian. She did not take to the ceremony of prim coffee-drinking with cakes from the bakery, or polite conversation about nothing in particular, occasionally laced with some premeditated reminiscence. Their meeting degenerated into grandmother shrieking hysterically, “Oy, Lise, I can’t understand what you are saying.” In Germany my grandmother ceased to speak German, because nobody could understand her archaic dialect. To make matters worse, Aunt Lise evidently felt she was a great benefactress who had rescued her country relatives from the steppes of Asia, while my parents were offended she had taken so long to get all the emigration documents in order, and had made not the slightest effort to ensure we did not end up in East Germany. For a while my mother was complaining several times a day that, for sentimental reasons, we had arranged our emigration through Aunt Lise rather than other relatives, who would have done it more quickly and effectively.

Russians were not popular in the Snow German villages of north Kazakhstan. Throughout my childhood I was told that Russians were pigs, drunkards, lazy and incompetent. Of course, the Kazakhs got it even worse. Life was not kind to the Germans, and they were not kind to anyone other than their animals and whichever family members they got on with.

Now everything has settled down. Aunt Lise still lives in Hamburg but we have not seen her again. My grandparents have gone back to Kazakhstan and I am going to Moscow. Shortly after the “reconciliation”, my grandfather told my father that if he did not help them to go back he would jump from the balcony of their “highly suitable” apartment. They had been saving up their German pensions for several months to pay for the return trip. Then they really did go back, bought themselves another dugout, and now they again get up at five every morning, gossip at their neighbors' fences, there are not enough hours in the day to get everything done, and my grandfather now has to sit a bit closer to the television because his eyesight is deteriorating and, in any case, he is now less fearful of the news because he knows they will die there. Nobody is going to deport or shoot them. It is the best place in the world. There, at the back of beyond, strawberries and pigeon-berries grow, and there every day, like a raincloud, the herd of cows goes out from the village, returning home at eventide. That is where I passed my childhood.

MARK

The Russian city rolled down to the river and elbowed its way into it on all fours, like an animal dying of thirst. A winter without stars, without thoughts, a gray mist like the tail of some ghostly predator. As we were riding to the hotel, I leaned my forehead against the bus window and saw in one of the squares a lone, meaningless monument, – a huge ball on a stick, with Russian lettering revolving over its surface. It looked like a statue of a Chupa Chups lollipop, as unreliable as everything else about this city, foolish but endearing. Since the day I dropped that note in the mailbox, and then lay floundering on the muddy pavement by my apartment block, I had been feeling a similar hollow space inside myself, as if I were an empty sphere covered with foil. I no longer had anything to lose or to fear. Someone on the plane said that you needed to be very careful. Beware of Russia! In fact the only difference here is that the light from the streetlamps is a bit different. They shine less brightly and tend to miss the street they're supposed to be illuminating. Or is it that the streets are trying to slither away from the jet of grimy orange light, the way fish in a television program about the underwater world dart away from the lamp of the cameraman in his flippers? You feel that if the temperature rose a little the town would melt and seep through pores in the earth along with the whole country. The ice cubes of the Kremlin would weep and disappear into puddles, rivers and swamps until there was no Russia left. Chupa Chups standing there in the square conveyed what was inside me. I gave it a friendly wink. It was the feeling you would have if you went to Africa and found a native playing with a plaster cast of your teeth.

I slept on the plane. Tearing myself free from the realm of Christine, I was flying to the tsardom of Andrey. I found that for me the globe was divided into two parts, and no matter which I was in, I would be the outsider. The road was full of potholes. The driver slowed down to avoid them, with intermittent success. Occasionally a wheel would fall into a water-filled pit. The feeling was indescribably delightful, evoking a childhood memory of my mother bouncing me on her knee. The city had some resemblance to Wiesbaden. A fat lady with a mane of hair sitting next to me said that she was given a terrible room when she attended a conference on something to do with Byzantium. She was wakened every hour by someone snoring in the room above. Every hour, she repeated, and there was no way to end her torment. A fellow passenger politely concurred. Almost all the passengers on the bus, even those who had been urging caution on the plane, declared without any obvious need that they loved Russia and were glad to be back. My neighbor with her redoubtable conferences on Byzantium (I wonder what secret hideaways they are held in) was no exception. She stretched luxuriously as she too proclaimed her satisfaction.

We got off the bus, collected our luggage and went in to the hotel foyer. At the door we were met by an extremely thin young woman with painted lips, who stood there smiling and periodically repeating, “Hello. Welcome to Voronezh!” Some people tried to greet her in Russian. It all looked pretty sad. When everyone was in she went with clattering heels behind the counter and began assigning us our rooms. There were several professors and they were entitled to single rooms. The young journalists were shepherded into doubles. I had not the slightest interest in who I might be living with; I knew none of the Byzantinists or young journalists and found myself sharing a room with the guy standing behind me in the line for registration. I just wanted to lie down.

The walls of the hotel were thick, the ceilings high, the stairs battered. The ants which had gnawed their way through the corridors were hardworking but relatively unskilled. Somehow you could hardly believe human beings had built this for other human beings. We proceeded down the corridors in triangular formation headed by an ugly girl in an apron who cleared a path to our room with her mooing and her ample figure. Behind came I and Mathias, whose name I had discovered from the register. He came from a small town in East Germany which ended in “-in” or “-ow”, like Russian surnames. On our progress we encountered an American who was drunk out of his mind, feeling his way along the wall and muttering something to himself about dancing. His words were like a prose version of the pop song “Baby, baby, do you wanna dance?” The door was opened to reveal a distance of about four meters between the beds. “Well, everything looks almost European,” Mathias said, and asked which bed I was going to sleep on. I looked around the room in search of a place where I could put you. If I lie on the right-hand bed I'll be able, without turning my head, to watch you lying on the wardrobe in your stockings and shifting your legs (as far as the space under the ceiling allows). Your tresses will tumble down over the wardrobe door but it will be unbearable if Mathias is standing there for ages putting his clothes in his compartment or whatever there is. I will choose the other bed and not dance with you, baby.

Half an hour later we were lying on the beds watching Russian television. A gray-haired man with a beard, his head trembling, was saying something in the hoarse voice of an alcoholic. The alcoholic and I looked into each other's eyes.

"Matze," I asked, "what brought you here?"

It turned out he was not only a young journalist but also a Slavist. I casually asked whether he was not perhaps an expert on Byzantium, and had the impression that after that question he looked at me with new respect. "Yes, yes," I said. "I have a lot of time for Byzantium. I think we should long ago have admitted it to the European Union instead of Turkey, within its eleventh-century boundaries, of course. And without any inhabitants. We can do without the Turks. We should re-populate Istanbul with Greeks. That's a brief outline of my project for reviving Byzantium." At least my idiotic plan contained the shadow of a great idea, but Matze was writing a thesis on Russian women's crime novels. Russian women, through their reading of crime novels, become emancipated and find their place in society, or something. I pictured a Russian woman reading a scene in which a body is dismembered and then refusing to make the soup for her husband's lunch smiling enigmatically in response to his reproaches, and clutching a gleaming knife behind her back.

I had a weird feeling. The hotel seemed populated by freaks, lunatics seeking the focus of their lives in the recycled trash of other people's cultures. I had every right to be here in their midst. The focus of my life, my love for you, was just as strange and useless and comical in its pointlessness, and yet that was the reel on which I wound the thread of my days. My love for Christine as a Reflection of the Polarity of a Diffuse System of Mnemonic Structures replicating the contours of your body, the smooth curve of your ear, the flower-scented hollow by your shoulder. By rights there should then have followed the swelling of your breast, but that was no longer available, your engorged nipple being currently in the mouth of that Russian. As soon as I intuited my kinship with the lunatics who had occupied this hotel, I felt a strange liking for the whole insane gaggle of them. I looked almost lovingly at the hopeless, lanky figure of the Slavist on the adjacent bed. I felt an urge to hit the town.

"Let's find somewhere to go for a drink, Matze."

We didn't know the city, it might be dangerous, we had to get up early, and he was already feeling tired. Before he had finished, I was closing the door behind me.

I was back in the hallway, immediately beyond which began the cold, infinite expanses of Russia, a succession of puddles with a thin lid of ice, rusting tractors belly up in ravines, a beautiful princess sitting by the corpse of a dragon with its heads chopped off, stroking them and weeping. I thought about the American we had met. Perhaps he had not been drunk, and was negotiating the hallway by leaning against the wall only because he needed something to hold on to in order not to be sucked into this strange world like a hapless snowflake. I felt a sudden urge to see him. We had encountered him on our floor, which meant he probably lived nearby, but I could hardly knock on all the doors until I found him. The stairs brought me down to reception, where the girl who greeted our group was playing cards on a computer, impaling kings and jacks on the needle of her mouse. Alongside, a plastic cup of tea was maturing nicely. I asked her which room the American on the third floor lived in, saying I had found something he had dropped in the hallway and wanted to return it.

"Was he drunked?"

"Yes."

"Room 308."

I knocked. For a couple of minutes there was no response, but as soon as I turned away the American appeared in the doorway in his shorts, squinting, having just got out of bed, and looking more sober than he had an hour previously. "Let's hit the town," I said. "The show must go on." I explained to the best of my ability that I was staying on this floor, had just arrived, and wanted to explore the city. It was not yet late, somewhere around half past midnight. When he understood the reason for my visit he was delighted: "We are the only two civilized people in this town!" he exclaimed, having first checked I was not Russian. "Let's go and get pissed. We'll show them how to live."

Five minutes later we emerged from the hotel. There are, he said, raising his arm, thousands of beautiful available Russian girls. His demeanor had something of the military commander about it. We set out over the eggy light spilt on the roadway by the streetlamps. The road was fairly lively. Shops were open, and at the crossroads one girl was repairing the mascara on the lashes of another, and Andreys were sloping around, locking their cars, going into their homes, drinking their beers. I felt I was an Andrey myself, having been dipped head first in the ink of the Russian night where all cats are black and all men are Andreys, and every one of them has formidable meat dangling between his legs. The American propositioned every girl we met, making use of his ten words of broken Russian. As a rule they remained indifferent to his efforts, brushing his hands away with a practiced movement. It looked like a dance, with him just progressing from one partner to the next. I watched his movements and began to feel a strange power over all these girls, as if I were standing in the circus ring with a whip in my hand and "Crack!" they would all shed their clothes and look obediently in the direction of me, Andrey, the boy with the golden flute who entices columns of young bodies to follow him, the one who can take you as his legitimate prey. But then you, watching me somewhere in a crystal ball, snapped your fingers and I no longer needed any of these girls.

What I did need was rubles. I bought them at a kiosk wallpapered with sheets of iron. Inside sat a bespectacled grandmother, like a snail in an armored shell, knitting a red sock. We walked past a few more houses. All around there was a curious amalgam of poverty and wealth. The city was a mixture of GDR-type concrete districts, the wealthier part of Wiesbaden, and what I expected Russia to look like, except that the streets were muddier. Next to the obligatory high-rise building with a tower (I'd seen one like this in Warsaw and on the emblem of the Moscow Olympics), I saw a church with a round dome which was unquestionably Byzantine, although I had no one with whom to share my joy at this discovery. Surrounded by bare, non-pedigree trees, a statue was sitting on a bench looking at his hands, counting his fingers or checking to see his metallic nails were properly polished. The American brought me to a club where women were swimming in the music like dolphins. In the parking lot outside there were several extremely expensive cars. I paid the entrance fee and slipped inside after the American, but he was moving at speed and, while I was checking my jacket, he vanished. What I was doing there was unclear. I did not want to dance, or pick up a girl, or to prove I can live without you because, baby, I can't. I was brought to this club by a river when I fell asleep thinking about you. When my pillow got wet, I woke up. The water was splashing Russian words; they flipped out of it like flying fish. Two mermaids walked past.

The attendant working in the cloakroom was a pale boy of fifteen or so with a hint of the vampire about him. The music hardly reached his cubbyhole. His long fingers probed my jacket for something to hang it up with. A drunken Russian was standing next to me. I looked at him. Matted hair fell over his forehead and he was covered in moles that looked like flies crawling over him. He lightly prodded my shoulder with his thumb and asked me something, with no suggestion of aggressiveness. I have difficulty understanding what happened next and can only say it was all over very quickly. I answered as best I could that I did not speak Russian. He said in English, "USA?" I answered "Germany". At this he came out with a long sentence in which I thought I heard the word "fascist". There was a dull thump, I felt a pain in my fist, and the Russian fell down. I had not hit him hard but he was drunk and lost his footing. I took a step back. The Russian was writhing about at my feet like a sea monster, trying to get up. Blood was dripping from his broken nose, leaving marks on the tiled floor like fiery planets. He muttered something quietly and tried to raise his body, but his foot kept sliding away as if he were lying on ice. His shoe lace was untied and snaked after his movements. I was at a loss as to what to do. I looked at the Russian's convulsive movements, then at the vampire cloakroom attendant, who just stood there with his mouth wide open, apparently preparing to sink his teeth into someone's neck. An instant later I realized that he was calling the security, whereupon someone behind lifted me in the air, dragged me to the exit, and I flew out into the street. A moment later the meathead bouncer reappeared and flung my jacket in the mud. I walked over and put it on. My visit to the nightclub had lasted a little over two minutes.

I stood at the entrance to the club in my muddy jacket, alone in an unfamiliar land, and the wet Russian night lay heavy on my shoulders like the paws of a bear. I somehow felt it was I, not the Russian, who had been punched in the face. The setting was out of a cheap American movie about the Russian mafia. I imagined a dozen Neanderthals emerging from the club with their Kalashnikovs at the ready. The Russian covered in moles would slowly raise a lighter to his cigarette, giving them the signal to open fire. Despite this premonition, I could not move. My idiotic crusade against the Russians had been successfully continued. First I had slept with a Russian, then I had punched a Russian. What would I do next? I could not even comfort myself that all this was in revenge for Christine, because if I should be taking revenge on anyone, it was her, but I still worship you, baby. It was obvious that these constant bust-ups with Russians could not just be coincidental, but it was hard to believe I myself was seeking out opportunities to get even with them. Oh Lord, how stupid! The sense of isolation that descended on me was cosmic and overwhelming. I do not doubt, my love, that you will never abandon me; part of you is forever connected, and when things get really bad for me your little heel will tingle, but right now... right now even you, my love, have covered your eyes with your fingers and blinked, making everything start jumping and shaking as if I were on a train. When I move my eyes from the areas dimly lit by streetlights to the areas dusty with darkness, I feel I have taken a leap. I would consent to your having invented me from start to finish, writing all sorts of nonsense about me in a red notebook with a velvet cover.

Something fell into my collar, a wet leech that lived on a cloud had jumped down and started drinking my blood. The door, which I was still watching, opened and out of the club there emerged, as I had expected, ten or so people. They did not, however, look like raging buddies of the guy I had floored in the cloakroom. Most of this party were girls, tall, slender, each pretty enough to be a model. Blonde tresses fell to their shoulders, and there was something about every one of them, a touch of the angel. Frankly, I've never seen more beautiful women. The girls were escorted by boys aged between eighteen and twenty in jackets and jeans, with trendy haircuts, dressed no doubt much as you might see young people dressed in London. But not in Germany. They passed through me like ghosts from a parallel world, etched in obliquely by the rain. Inexplicably, the American had worked his way into their group. In his hand he held an almost full bottle of vodka. He was swaying, and alongside these Russians looked provincial. Nevertheless, he recognized me, came over and began tugging at my jacket sleeve, yelling, "Come and join us. We're going to have fun. We're going to have a party!" The Russians and their girls sat themselves in the expensive cars I had noticed scattered haphazardly before I went into the club, like shoes removed and thrown down anywhere by visitors. I took a few steps and got in the back seat of the latest Audi with the American and one of the angels. I forbade myself to think about what I was doing. In any case, it made no sense to carry on standing in the rain.

The driver was a Russian, maybe nineteen years old. He appeared to be very drunk and was very handsome. A blonde got in beside him who had an exquisite mermaid's ear, like a seashell from a beach on the Mediterranean. A green fairy dangled from it, swinging its legs. I did not get a good look at her face. Her hand was resting on the Russian boy's thigh. He slammed into reverse and within seconds we were racing at a crazy speed after the other cars. No one seemed surprised that I had appeared. The angel sitting between me and the American turned her eyes towards me and in a trusting, childish way laid her head on my shoulder. We overtook muddy Ladas of the night. If there were any road markings they had disappeared under the slush. I had a feeling we were careering along on the wrong side of the road. The American opened the window and shouted something at the cars we were overtaking. The only word I could make out was "motherfucker". I began to feel scared and, reaching cautiously so that the angel leaning on my shoulder should not open her eyes, I took the vodka bottle out of the American's hands. The lips so close to mine smelled of sour berries: currants or cranberries. The vodka tasted vile, assuredly no better than the gasoline we were burning up as we flew through the dark streets. I had no idea that vodka could be drunk in large gulps like this. To do so you need only to be hurtling down the wrong side of the road in the city of Voronezh with a cranberry-scented angel by your side. Within a minute I had drunk roughly half the bottle.

My insides were on fire, but it did not matter. I

discovered that vodka is a magic fluid which evokes love. I could see it once more, except that now the flame coming from my chest was not blue but bright red. I loved the slanting rain, the dirty water drenching us from below and from above and washing away our anger and hatred and stupidity. I loved Russians because they are not afraid of death, and because generation after generation they give birth to angels who will snuggle up to absolutely anybody in the back seat of a German car. We sped past the lunatic monument to Chupa Chups and I sent it my love, which made it spin like a top and fly up into the sky. Then I turned my head and pressed my lips to the cranberry angel. She never opened her eyes but turned her body full on to me and began to moan. I supped her juices, trying to catch her tongue with mine while, on the other side, the American was stroking her ass. Breaking away from the angel, I took a few more gulps, love burst out of me in a fountain of flames. The inside of the car was literally on fire, we were all engulfed in flames. I dropped the empty bottle to the floor and passed out, reduced to ashes.

I have no reliable information on the ensuing seven or eight hours. I probably came to from time to time, but it is difficult to know whether what I saw around me was real or simply part of my imagination. Physically, I felt very ill the whole time, but in my heart I was happy as never before. Sometimes when I opened my eyes, I saw glowing orange creatures which loved me hovering above. I came to my senses in an empty, spacious room, lying on my side, engulfed in a downy duvet and with a smile on my lips. There was a fireplace in the wall opposite and the last orange specter took fright, slipped into it and vanished. I got up immediately and staggered over, obsessed by an idea from my dream but, as I was on my way, it melted and by the time I reached the fireplace I had quite forgotten why I had wanted to go there. Strangely enough, though, my jacket was in the fireplace. It had had a rough night and was now even muddier. The rest of my clothes were on me, except for my shoes which had been placed neatly by the bed. They had been cleaned and polished, which exceeded every measure of absurdity I'd hitherto known. I searched the pockets of my jeans and found my wallet and rubles intact. I had had to pay only for entry to the nightclub. I heard steps. Someone was walking overhead. I looked around the room and, except for me, thank God, there was no one. It was sumptuously but ridiculously decorated, with a huge clock and animal skins on the walls. Turning to look around it produced a terrible headache.

I just wanted to get to the hotel as soon as possible and take a shower. I had no idea where I was. All I could see through the window were strange, bare trees descending to the river. It was unbearable to think about yesterday. By the time I reached the fireplace I'd more or less remembered what had happened, at least up to the moment we began drinking vodka in the car: the cranberry lips, the American. Now I just wanted to put as much distance between me and that as possible, and the sooner the better. I pulled on my shoes and cautiously slipped out of the room. There was a foyer beyond, one of the doors of which undoubtedly led outside. Hesitating for a moment (the thought flashed through my mind to go in search of a shower), I decided not to push my luck and leave while I could do so unnoticed. Outside, I looked up at the house. It was a large three-story cottage of dull red brick, halfway between a down-at-heel castle and a train shed. Try as I might, I could not remember entering it on my own two feet. Looking around, I saw that the whole district was covered in similar houses which squatted like fat hens all over the hill, at the bottom of which a wide, pregnant river was sleeping.

I walked up a muddy sand track and five minutes later saw you standing next to a rusty pipe which was sticking vertically out of the ground. The pipe had a lever on which you had hung a metal bucket. You brought down your hand and water hissed into it. You were wearing a checkered coat and funny brown wellington boots too big for your feet. Above these your legs were bare. You looked at me and water began overflowing from the bucket, making your wellingtons shiny. It flowed down to me, licked me with its tongue and ran on down, driving the chickens off their hill, flooding the city of Voronezh, and then the whole world, leaving only you and me. All our lives we would now have to wear wellington boots and the ground would squelch under us when we made love. You would lean against a tree, the only one left which, naturally, would be the Tree of Life and whimper, "Oh Gott!"

You asked if I was thirsty, then unhesitatingly poured almost all the water in the bucket out on the ground. You handed me the rest and I drank eagerly. For some reason you were laughing and constantly repeating something I could not understand because I'd been in Russia for too long and lost touch with you and our language. Then you poured out water for me and I washed my hands and face, until my hands began to ache with the cold and you filled up the bucket again and went away, opening and closing the gate to the Garden of Eden behind you. There were twisted, bare apple trees growing in there, and an old silent dog in love with the smell of your wellington boots nudged you with his nose.

Soon I reached the main road and could see the city gradually beginning to the right. One car after another was headed that way. I raised my hand, hoping someone would stop but immediately realized I had forgotten the name of my hotel. More precisely, I did not think I had ever known it. A moment later, an unshaven man in a Volkswagen pulled up. He had two crates of green tomatoes in the back. I explained in English and German that I needed to get to the city center. He nodded and showed me the price on the display of his mobile phone. There was music playing in the car; a Russian singer with a sly, disagreeable voice was doing his best with a very dull tune. Along the roadside were buckets of potatoes over which babushkas in identical woolen shawls stood sentinel. After my encounter with you, a curious serenity came over me, as if I were being passed from hand to hand like some precious, fragile object, a crystal swan perhaps, by a succession of angels. The whole progress bringing me to this car, which might have seemed random and meaningless, had actually long been predestined. What coincidence could explain my encounter on the path with your double, your Russian shadow, your reflection in the chilly Russian air, the way Voronezh reflected parts of Wiesbaden?

The buckets of potatoes disappeared and we entered the outskirts of the city proper: grimy, cheerless houses built without an identity of their own but which had acquired one, a hideous identity, under the action of time. They were studded with the fans of air conditioners; here and there new white window frames had been inserted like patched-up shell holes on a sinking ship. I looked out for the hotel, or at least a street I might have come across when walking around yesterday, but while I was asleep they had changed the scenery. I was grateful when we at least drove into one of the Wiesbaden districts and the city became more attractive. A little later we drove into a large square, in the center of which a banner was hanging over the glass facade of a wide building. It read, in German, "Voronezh Welcomes the Russo-German Forum of Young Journalists." I asked the driver to stop and paid him. He muttered something, turned to the back seat and handed me a large green tomato. I headed for the building, reasoning that they should at least be able to tell me the name of the hotel at which conference guests were staying.

Inside, behind a dusty glass partition, a girl with vertical hair transfixed by a long hairpin, rather as I imagine one mounts butterflies, was flirting with the security guard, who gave me a surly look. I remembered yesterday's nightclub and thought that perhaps I really was beginning to look dangerous. Whatever it was, I presented my passport and press card. The girl examined them carefully, checked something on her list, and invited me to follow her. We went up to the second floor and before I could ask her anything, she opened the door in front of me and went back downstairs to her guard. I took a step forward and found myself in a room with a huge oval table around which all our Byzantinists were seated. Our whole absurd, besuited bunch of freaks (including several professors) sat there gawping at me and perhaps also at the huge green tomato I held in my outstretched hand, as if proffering it to the meeting.

It was a challenging moment, but one I could rise to. I paused for an instant before biting into the tomato. Green juice trickled down my arm, making the insides of my sleeve sticky. There was an empty seat at the table. I walked across the room and took it, having ascertained that a card bearing my name identified it as mine. The conference program, which I had not read, was lying at this moment in my apartment on the thirteenth floor, on that very couch on which we... did it for the first time. I'd thrown the blue booklet down on it and left for Russia, totally uninterested in what activities might be planned for me in a city whose name I could not even pronounce. I regretted that now. I really should have been able to foresee that, even on the first day, something would have been organized. In front of our group, over by the wall, several Russians and a translator were making a less than cutting-edge presentation. I could tell they were pleased to see me and one, rather portly, even gave me a wink. The Byzantinists looked at me in horror and whispered among themselves. I hardly had the appearance of a worthy representative of our federal republic with its Kantzlerin who looks like a deep-frozen fish. My jacket had marked the seat and my shoes, polished by elves in the night, had regained a layering of clay. I was unshaven, and doubtless had rings under my eyes and yellow blotches and who knows what else that could be discerned if you peered at me as intently as the gray-haired professors in collar and tie sitting across from me were doing. The Russian with a face the color of a lemon, – what did you get up to last night, then, colleague? – whose paper my arrival had interrupted, resumed his speech while I ruminatively finished my tomato, wondering how best to extricate myself from this situation. My fellow passenger from the bus was occupying the next seat (our names probably began with the same letter) and disapprovingly slipped a tissue under the table to me.

I was soon finding the proceedings entertaining. The translator was clearly struggling. The only words she pronounced clearly were "Journalismus" and "international". Everything else got scrambled by her accent, and what little could be heard made no sense or was horrendously banal. As far as I could tell, the speaker was the Dean of the Department of Journalism at the local university. The portly gentleman next to him represented the gas company, and another sleek individual was either the mayor or his deputy. The interpreter was a very pretty girl with a little round face. In her fluffy knitted cardigan with huge gingerbread buttons she resembled a cat. She stood looking scared in the midst of them, purring out the translation in a language only faintly reminiscent of German. I thought that in the break all us men in this room with its unendurable red curtains should take her on our knees in turn and tickle her behind the ear.

As far as I could tell, the Russians were giving us a polite ear-bashing to the effect that the task of modern journalism was to promote mutual understanding between countries while we were engaging solely in anti-Russian propaganda which, it was hinted, sei nicht gut. We were writing all sorts of horror stories about Russia, about wars in the Caucasus, the murder of journalists and the absence of freedom of speech, when everything was really quite different and they had vast fields here spread, like butter, with wheat, above which thousands of rockets were taking off into space and orbiting cardboard stars from each of which there smiled a black and white Gagarin. The war was over, the dead Caucasians buried, and from the breast of each a mountain had grown which pierced white clouds from which milk ran down its slopes. Khodorkovsky in the uranium mines was glowing with remorse for having incommoded the state, which meant that at night his fellow inmates could not sleep because it was too bright and they had to cocoon him in a blanket and one day he would hatch into a butterfly with oil-black wings and fly following the smell of grass toward the star on the Kremlin to publicly impale itself on one of its sharp points and thereby solve his country's problem. It was just as I arrived at this image that my hangover caught up with me.

The oval table was a lake on which were scattered the islets of papers, and you were sailing on it in your little boat. Every man round the table kept whispering, whispering words of love to you and wanted you tied up at his bollard, but you just smiled, lowering your eyes, and picked the mother-of-pearl river lilies and put them in the bottom of your boat until it looked like a pastry. Above you, like a cloud, Russian words scudded by, and, of course, "Journalismus" and "international" because without them the conference would not have been a conference, but they were of no concern to you because they were boring and ugly, and when you're sitting in your boat you can feel the coolness of its smooth wooden surface with your butt. You row the water with your hands and slide your toes over the lily stems in the bottom of the boat, and there is just nothing more important in life than that. All I am is a journalist from the very tidiest country in the world, where people write badly of this other country, big, muddy and weird, whose rulers have grown rich on the sale of the fluid that flows through its subterranean veins. Now this country is berating me in the tones of a woman who has sold a kidney and half her blood to buy a diamond necklace. It is, of course, the same money on which I was invited here and, of course, if I am going to keep talking politics your butt is not going to feel anything at all, nothing touching it, nothing cool, so let's forget politics.

I went out to the toilet and spent a long time splashing cold water on my face. The me-through-the-looking-glass tried not to look at the me on this side of it. The green tomato in my stomach reconstituted itself and started slowly to rotate. I puked into the toilet, sluiced myself again and went back to the Byzantinists, waited for the fat gas man to finish his speech, and put up my hand.

Criticizing Russia is no different from kicking a tethered bear: no matter where you aim, you will end up kicking its soft belly where there is nothing except that soft, defenseless gut almost the size of a continent which sucks your foot in. I took the floor and for ten minutes kicked the bear, repeating words everybody has heard a thousand times before, which have always been said when anyone is talking about Russia. I spoke slowly, then waited for Pussycat to translate what I had said, then continued. It was as if the two of us were meowing a wonderful song about a totally dire country in which there was absolutely no freedom of speech or purring. When I finished, a concerned Byzantinist I did not know put up his hand and said that in my speech I had been expressing only my personal opinion, which by no means represented the opinion of the group as a whole, and then delivered a load of bullshit about cooperation and development. Oh, sure, I thought. A lot you write about cooperation in your newspapers. For some reason it is a whole lot more about polonium. If the Byzantinists had previously been looking at me reproachfully, they appeared now to view me with superstitious horror, as if I were some kind of ghoul. My feelings can be conveyed by the following metaphor: it was as if I were being awarded the Order of Distinguished Enemy of Russia, in the Kremlin. The Russians listened to us a bit longer, looking bored. I think they had been expecting speeches like mine. Then the Dean said a few words I did not understand because they did not include "Journalismus", or "international", and we were invited into the next room for lunch.

The table was so piled with food that your boat was crushed between the salads and its splinters were used as toothpicks. You were saved by Andrey and hastened to repay the favor by taking off your clothes. You were so eager you could not do it quickly enough. "How much fucking do you need, slut?" he said and I stuck a fork in him, cut him up with my knife, and swallowed him in large chunks. Matze was seated beside me and, almost in tears, asked why I so hated Russia and why I had to create an international incident. "They killed my grandfather at Stalingrad," I said, and looked out the window where flour was being sprinkled from the sky. "Has it never occurred to you to ask what he was doing at Stalingrad? Stalingrad, you know, is nowhere near Berlin, or even East Prussia." Matze was clearly intent on re-educating me. I stared him straight in the eyes and, covering my mouth, said my grandfather had been saving humanity from the Jewish-Bolshevik Conspiracy. Nobody else tried to engage me in conversation, except for one professor who, as we were leaving the building, told me I was a disgrace to the delegation and all young German journalists. "Aim higher," I corrected him. "Not only German journalists, but the whole of 'internationaler Journalismus'."

The Byzantinists went off to see the sights of the city, and their guide was none other than Pussycat, who trod on the flour as softly and carefully as if touching the keys of a piano. She was walking at the front of the group and soon, unfortunately, was lost to view beyond people's backs. I went back to the hotel. My grandfather was not killed at Stalingrad. I lied. He was captured there by the Russians and never returned. What difference does that make?

Fifty transparent rivulets ran over me, came together at my feet in a minor sea and, when I turned off the water, gurgling peevishly, drained through a round orifice along with all its dolphins, whales and ships which had been too late to discover the local America. After my shower, I sprawled on my stomach in bed, my face buried in the chicken feather pillows. Would those pillows remember it? How many people must have left their faceprints there. I fell asleep and dreamed another of my Byzantine dreams. I am in Turkey, sitting in some dodgy diner, and on the table in front of me is a teapot of unusual design. A glass tube spirals upwards. One end is immersed in a herbal decoction while the other is outside the teapot. A gray-haired Turk tells me I am an air bubble in the tube and asks which way I want to go, into the teapot or out of it. I detect a catch in this, but life in an enclosed teapot strikes me as intolerable and I choose to move up the tube and out, but before I can answer the Turk, I am back in Russia. Damn! My room is empty. I want to give my answer but it is already too late. The Turk has gone.

I have nowhere to go. I've had enough of adventures with the American and my headache has come back. It feels like I have a pile-driver concentrating on my temples. Remember how I used to fly, lying next to you, naked, exhausted, wrung out. For takeoff I have only to push away from your body, perform a certain number of movements, I seem to release a spring, and then be still, my mouth open, silent, like a fish, saying words of some sort, poetry in a tongue I never knew, something Byzantine again, I expect, and at the same time you push me hard with your own hands, grazing my skin, tossing me up millions of kilometers into space. You told me afterwards that during orgasm you fall down and down to a realm beneath the bed, perhaps even to the center of the earth, where like the reflection of a candle in a Christmas bauble your love for me once burned. Now through my universe, where on every planet my palm prints are ablaze (where I have tried to push myself off from them in order to get back to you) the Russian cosmonaut Andrey is flying on his twenty-centimeter rocket.

Matze comes back and tells me the whole group is about to go to the theater. I stump over to my suitcase to get clean clothes. He abruptly turns on the light and I close my eyes because they hurt. In the darkness I feel in the suitcase for my pants and sweater, your breasts, your hips, your lips which hungrily nuzzle my fingers. I get dressed and ask the Slavist what it is we're going to see. Chekhov. In Russian, of course. We wait downstairs for all the young journalists and all the professors of Byzantine Studies who have come along for the ride. I stand apart, shaven, well-built, with the imprint of your lips on my pants, ready for war but, thank God, no one comes near me. In the bus taking us to the theater I sit alone. The fat woman has decamped to the other end of the bus. Before the show, the Russians ply us with champagne in a separate room. All the alcoves and ins and outs in it are concealed by gilded molding, as if the architect could not abide sharp edges. The bubbles in the glasses, like me in my dream, want to rise to heaven. I begin to feel sick again.

On the stage Russian nobles drank tea in the orchard. Now and again one of them would get out of his chair and go away or come back and immediately start saying something very excitedly, waving his arms about. Their women said little, toyed with fans, and were obviously very bored. During the intermission, the head of the Byzantinists informed me that the Russian side had withdrawn my accreditation for all conference events and that the morning after next I would be sent home early. I had supposedly wrecked the opening session of their conference, turned up drunk, and insulted Russia. I feel wickedly amused, as if finally I was getting out of the teapot I was dreaming about and moving up the spiral glass tube. I drank three glasses of champagne to the health of the Emperor Constantine, and after the break sat down next to the pussycat interpreter, who had not abandoned our group of lunatics even in the theater. Her body warmed my shoulder, as if under her blouse she were harboring a supply of warm milk. Far away on the stage, a bald nobleman crashed to his knees before his lady, startling the first rows of the audience, while I leaned over to whisper in her ear that she was looking very beautiful. From further whisperings I learned that it was actually the Byzantinists who'd been most anxious to get rid of me. She translated their conversation with the Russians on the subject of my misconduct. Unsurprisingly, the Russians had not insisted on my continued presence, but left to their own devices would probably not have insisted on expelling me either. "Don't be upset." "Sei bitte nicht traurig." She said it so simply and naturally, as if she had unbuttoned her blouse, pulled out her breast and let me drink my fill of her milk. Then I told her a bit about my hometown. When we were not talking about anything complicated, I could follow her German.

Christine, just come and do not torment me. Come if only for a moment, baby, like that time when I was sitting with my eyes closed in front of the suitcase. Come as a ghost, a cloud, a vision, a stranger, a thousand times a stranger, mauled by other men, fucked by other men, just come and do not torment me. The curtain rushed to the sides, like eyelids opening, and you were right there in the pupil, on the thirteenth floor, in front of my door. You leaned a sheet of paper against the wall and wrote me a note which downstairs you would have to drop in my mailbox because I am not at home. I am, can you believe it, at present in Russia. I will come, read it, go up in the elevator and cook pasta in my little apartment, and your words will flutter all through it like butterflies. I will shoo them away from the boiling saucepan. Could this happen? Okay, I know.

But something I know for a fact is that, since the Earth is round and I am several thousand kilometers away, I am standing at an angle relative to you, and who else would I measure angles relative to? That means everything around here is askew from birth, and the buildings go up already off perpendicular. Thank God I'll be flying away from here the day after tomorrow, assuming that passenger planes can take off from an inclined surface.

After the theater Matze and I went back to our room, closed the door, turned off the lights, and found ourselves in an empty black box out of which morning pulled us as a conjuror might pull out rabbits. It had snowed all night. Matze went off with the rest of them to the next session. I, of course, had been crossed off all lists, sat on the bed and fiddled aimlessly with my watch, which I had obdurately not changed to Russian time. I turned on the television and hopped channels. A succession of talking heads followed each other on the screen and, as I did not understand a word, it seemed to me that the whole lot of them, even the children's cartoons from the Byzantine era, were singing the praises of Putin.

Russia has its own time. The minutes there do not go round in a circle the way they do in Germany, but fall like peas, from up to down. When there are enough of them, the bowl upends and for a while a person falls into a crazy parallel world where there is no time. I experienced something of the kind on the first day I arrived. So now I was sitting in my room, reading a copy of *Spiegel* I had found on Mathias's bed. The windows were blinded by snow, tap-tap, – that was the peas rattling, and I had the feeling there was something I had not got round to doing in Russia. Of course, I was not in the least sorry not to be taking part in their inane conference; sooner or later I would have got kicked out of it anyway. Rather, there was some small detail missing which I needed if I were to understand something very important. How can I explain it to you, baby? A corner of the painting was still white.

At two in the afternoon I was invited down to lunch. None of our group had yet returned and I was alone in the dining room, apart from a group of Hungarians or Romanians. One of them kept fishing things out of his soup and piling them up next to his plate. I went back to my room, packed my bag, lay down, again started reading the magazine, and sank deeper and deeper into the bed. It sucked me down like a marsh and, when I felt I was about to get completely stuck, I got up and went to look for the American. I knocked at his door in vain. Returning to my own room I was almost pleased to find Matze there. He pulled out a laptop, deciding to work this evening. I nearly sat back down on the bed, but knew I was fired up and could not stop now. My eye fell on the conference program. I picked it up and discovered that Pussycat was called Tatyana Golubkina: her name and photo were there in the list of organizers. Grabbing the brochure, I went down to Reception, where the same girl was still sitting glued to a monitor. Within twenty minutes, having several times landed on pornography websites, she winkled Pussycat's address out of the Internet and wrote it down for me.

When I came out of the hotel, it was completely dark. Everything above the level of the buildings had been hastily daubed with murky paint, the way they obscure windows in the toilets here. No prickly stars were going to get through it. I took the taxi on duty at the entrance, gave the driver Pussycat's address, and watched us slowly pull away from the curb. I felt a strange rush of excitement. Once again I was speeding through Voronezh at night with no goal in mind, no plan, only a vague feeling that I must not waste my last cold, wet, beautiful night in Russia, which had lain down so obediently at my feet.

By the time ten minutes passed we had left behind the concrete boxes and were driving into a rural part of the city, or a village on the outskirts. I don't know. The lights burning in the windows of the wooden houses made you feel gutted. Women carrying bags were walking on the sidewalks and disappearing behind fences. The car passed aimlessly through side streets. Every crack in the roadway had been stuffed with snow. The driver twice asked passersby for directions before, finally, we turned into a desolate lane and stopped near a two-story wooden house. He waved his hand toward it, I paid him, got out and walked to the porch. I had to bang on the door as there was no bell, and it was opened by a woman of forty-five or so who was holding a yellow bowl. I said syllable by syllable, "ta-tya-na go-lub-kin-a", managing to convey that I did not speak Russian. The woman was terribly taken aback but tried to communicate something through gestures, and I understood that Pussycat was not here at present but not far away either and I could walk there. I asked her to draw me a map, she tore off a strip of newspaper, sketched several lines with arrows and thrust it into my hand. I thanked her and left.

The first arrow led me back to the end of the lane. There were lights far away, but it was dark and my feet sank into the snow. Nevertheless, the whole situation was giving me an inexplicable buzz. I almost ran in the direction indicated by the arrows. At a crossroads I slipped and fell and my hand was burned by snow as sharp as glass. I was running in some lost world on the edge of nowhere surrounded by the polar night and wooden houses and only very occasionally encountering passersby and cars. On all sides dogs were barking, driven crazy by the snow and their own loneliness. I first ran past No. 35, a house as irredeemably wooden as all the others, stopped at No. 39 and had to count back two houses. It had a bell and the door was opened by a young guy. He had short cropped hair, an indefinably Asiatic face, and was wearing sweatpants and a shirt. I repeated my trick of pronouncing Pussycat's name. He eyed me darkly and let me in. I took off my sodden shoes and followed him through a room with the television on to the kitchen, where Pussycat in a neat apron was frying potatoes. The character in the sweatpants stood behind me with his arms folded but, when he heard me speaking German, went back to the other room. At first Pussycat simply did not recognize me, and then could not believe I had so straightforwardly landed in on her. I said I was flying back tomorrow and wanted to say goodbye, knowing that did not sound very convincing when we had only once talked at the theater. She asked me to wait, went out, then came back and invited me to have dinner with them. Pussycat was living in this wooden house with her boyfriend.

"I will cook now, and you please wait with him in the room," she said. I did as I was told.

We sat together on the couch. He was watching football on the television. He was slightly shorter than me, looked like a Mongol, a solidly built guy in a gray T-shirt. For a while we said nothing, keeping the ball in midfield. Then, without even a click, the television turned off. With the remote in his hand, he looked at me, then got up and closed the door to the corridor.

"Why you are here?" He spoke English, very bad English, to me, but everything was perfectly clear even without words, I had hit rock bottom, the ultimate goal of my journey.

"A Russian took my girl," I replied. "Girl. She was with me. We love each other. Russian comes. She goes with him."

"Who do this?"

For a moment I did not reply.

"You."

"I?" He was not sure he had understood me correctly. He frowned, trying to grasp the mental construct which had caused me to come here to watch football with him.

"Yes. You."

"You want to fight?" he asked.

"Yes," after which it was simplicity itself to find a common language. We went out to the yard, and I immediately slipped in the snow. With difficulty, my hands kept sinking into a snowdrift, I got on all fours before he kicked me in the chest and I fell again. I rolled in a ball away from Andrey, I think I can call him that, got to my feet and climbed out of the other side of the snowdrift, which we now had between us. He was about twenty meters away, a dark, almost invisible figure. The streetlights were a long way off, and he made no move.

"Hey, Russky," I said to him, floundering through the snow. The snow got everywhere because our German clothing is crap. We no longer have to walk through snow or carry water home in buckets. I made my way through the snow very slowly, so I caught him by surprise when, setting foot on solid ground, I rushed at him. Andrey nevertheless reacted swiftly. He drew back his fist to strike, but the ground was slippery and I could not stop. I shoved rather than hit him. He slipped and we both fell, he on his back, banging his head on the ice (I heard the clunk), and I fell almost on top of him. This evidently enraged him, because he all but snarled, although they were still human words, if clearly not addressed to me. Perhaps he was invoking some gods of Russia. (Remember those images of round creatures on the jars in Nina's house!) He pushed me away and began quickly getting to his feet. I got up even faster, because I knew that given the chance he would give me a good kicking. When he came at me, we were both on our feet.

I let a punch through to my face but, fending him off, also hit him, lightly, sideways, but with both hands. The next instant I avoided another blow, retreated and fell backwards into the snowdrift I had just got out of. A thought came through to me at just the wrong moment and would not let go. Flat on my back, I did not see him coming up, I only heard the crunch of snow under his shoes. The sky was clear and calm, no aircraft, no sound from above. He didn't kick me. For some reason he was waiting for me to get up. I did so, and turned my back on him, not looking round and heading right into the middle of the snowdrift. I no longer wanted to fight. More or less in the middle of the snowdrift he caught up with me and pushed me down, face first in the snow. I fell into it, turned my head to breathe, and stayed there lying inside a great heap of snow. I was almost enjoying myself, floating in weightlessness. Because of the cold, probably, I was not feeling any pain, although he had clearly given me a good drubbing.

Then I began to expand. For a minute one vision, one image, had me in thrall. The Russian came toward me, holding your hand and – gave it to me. Simply gave it to me, without a fight. I took your cold hand and led you away. It seemed to me that there, inside that mountain of snow, I had understood something. In the history of our relationship, Andrey was an essential link. He had to make you at least a little bit Russian so that we can be together, because I too am Russian. I am Russian myself. I am a Russian. He was readying you for me. The bastard. By sleeping with you, by kissing you. There was no other way. We were not happy as we were. Our happiness was born in Russia. It crawled out of a Russian jar, round and with an idiotic smile. “Eat me!” it squealed.

I heard Pussycat come running out and start yelling at her boyfriend. I think she even tried to hit him. He was mumbling something in a monotone, trying to justify his actions. “God!” I thought. “Who am I fighting? Who am I trying to destroy?” The fire went out of me. I started to feel cold. I slowly extricated myself from the snowdrift. Where my face had been the snow was covered in black marks. I ran a hand over my face and realized my nose was bloody and broken. Sinking in the snow and waving my arms about like the walking trees in *Lord of the Rings*, I emerged from the snowdrift. Pussycat and the Russian were silent. He pushed the girl behind him and got ready to fight me again but now everything had changed. “Stop!” I said, spreading my arms wide. “Stop!” They looked at me in such puzzlement that I burst out laughing. “Gut, Gut, Iwan!” I declared, slapping him on the shoulder. “Idiot,” he said, maybe in German but probably in Russian. It no longer mattered. “Let’s go and eat,” Pussycat said bemused. “Dinner is ready.” She went off, keeping herself wrapped in a gray shawl. We waddled after her like geese, our shoulders bumping in the narrow porch.

In the hallway we tried to take off our shoes. Here, in the warmth, I began fully to feel the pain. It started in my hands with my twisted fingers. They were covered in blood too, as if they had been through a meat grinder. The Russian was cursing, fingering the back of his head where it had hit the ice.

"Do not tell her," he said in English, then took me by the chin and examined my face. He smiled and said something again. He pointed to a door behind which I found the bathroom. There was only cold water but that didn't matter. I writhed, and writhed again periodically as I washed the blood away, my heart pounding at my temples. I came out ten minutes later when I had re-learned, just about, how to move my limbs. The Russian was sitting smugly at a table laden with food: stew, potatoes, two kinds of lettuce (one incongruously red), sauerkraut, pickled cucumbers and tomatoes. In the middle stood a bottle of vodka. I pointed at it and he poured me a glass, I drank it and, with a glance toward the kitchen from which there came the clatter of dishes, he refilled it. I downed that one too, then fished out a piece of meat, quickly chewed and swallowed it. By the time Pussycat arrived there were three full glasses waiting and I was smiling blissfully. It was not the warmth or the feeling of intoxication which wiped the pain from my body like a warm damp sponge. The war was over.

The peace which had come to this snowy place exploded now and again in a firework volley of barking dogs. Peace flung its ancient splendors over all the earth, and I was not surprised when the table was lit up by a blue flame bursting from my heart.

I went back to the hotel in a taxi. Pussycat's boyfriend spent five minutes chatting to the driver. They both laughed, looking in my direction, but it was all the same to me. I needed to be back home, getting ready to meet you again, baby. Who knows what adventures might have befallen you in the meantime? I closed my eyes and sighed deeply, surprised now that I could have been so stupid. I should have guessed long ago. The whole problem could be expressed as a simple mathematical equation. I knew the basic condition is that you and I had to be equal; that in front of the "equals" sign there was me, as vast as the cosmos, giving out a matte blackness. Mark, Markovsky, Markov, Markin. On the other side was you, suspended in space, glowing. But no, in order to convince myself that our love was infinite I had to stage my own Stalingrad. For a moment I feared I'd left something terribly important in that snowdrift, but then shrugged and decided that I didn't care even if they found my skin there in the spring and buried it under a wooden Russian cross. I had no more time to waste. I needed to get back to you.

Mathias took a look at my face and muttered something disapproving. I staggered over to my bed, showed him the middle finger and promptly, without undressing, fell asleep. In the morning I'm flying back to Germany.

VALERIA

Expectedly, that episode of the crazy girl threatening Christine only brought her closer to Andrey. Finding herself in a situation where she had to fight to keep the man she loved, she had in retrospect to recognize the value of what it was she had to fight for. It was not the relationship itself, but the fact that she had to endure distress because of it (which by German standards was very considerable) that provided her with clear evidence of the existence of a major love affair. That night, when I tried to comfort her in our Russian courtyard and her mobile phone kept ringing every fifteen minutes, she had eventually, at about four in the morning, answered it. She spoke briefly, and fell asleep on the sofa. Almost immediately, circling once round the yard, a BMW screeched to a halt under my windows. Andrey, very calm, fresh and focused, took her in his arms and carried her down to the car. He just said hello to me as he walked past into the room, found Christine by himself and, as he left, quietly said thank you. He evidently believed that I had inclined her to make peace and had told her something that made her forget the incident of the threats.

Afterwards Christine came to the cafe a few times again, at first with the redhead. For some reason Nina was no longer one of their crowd. Then she would come in alone or with a couple of new, amazingly colorless friends. Christine seemed increasingly isolated from them all. If anyone could have supported her it was only Nina, herself caught between two worlds, but unfortunately Nina had disappeared. Red-haired Silke seemed to make no attempt to conceal her irritation over her friend's caprice. Andrey did not fit her idea of a nice, amusing foreign loser. He was part of an arrogant, self-assured force which, paying no attention to anyone else, altered German cities to its own needs. Under Silke's classification he counted as macho, an invader who didn't give a toss about the culture of the country in which he was doing so well. And then there was the matter of his involvement in the war in Chechnya. He seemed to have no regrets, was not ashamed, did not engage in political debate with Silke, and evidently no bloodstained boys disturbed his dreams. In short, his behavior fell far short of what might have been expected of a decent immigrant. Silke, of course, had nothing against immigrants as such. That left me, if only for a time as I would shortly be on my way to Moscow. New tenants had been found for my apartment, my parents' basement every week gave houseroom to several more boxes of my stuff. On one occasion Christine and Andrey decided to come and visit me. I went round to a Japanese store, bought some sheets of nori, some rice, wasabi in a tube, and a bottle of sake. In happier times of my relationship with Ralf we had taken a course in Frankfurt to learn how to prepare sushi. I also concocted some cream balls to a recipe of my mother's, but before I had time to add the filling the doorbell rang.

The day was really frosty. I barely managed to force myself out for my morning jog. It had not snowed but there was a white fur covering everything, so that when my guests arrived I went off like a real Japanese wife to warm the sake in a saucepan. The first moments were awkward. Both of them seemed a little embarrassed by their partner. Andrey and I struggled a bit, switching from Russian to German and sticking with German in the end. After a while, when they had drunk the sake, they warmed up on the couch and Christine gave a comical frown and asked whether there was some mysterious reason why Russians liked the most disgusting drinks on the planet. A little later I got them to make the sushi rolls. Andrey's were a sight for sore eyes, while Christine's kept falling apart. Everything became more relaxed, and you could believe that Russians and Germans were perfectly capable of creating a successful union, if not very often, and that a mannish German girl could flower into a delicate lily behind the back of a soldier who had relocated to Germany. Finally, when all the rolling was finished, we began to eat and Andrey told us that during the war he often imagined two girls in a warm, peaceful flat spooning a variety of delicacies into his mouth. "Did you ever imagine that while doing so they would be speaking German?" I asked. He said that in his dream nobody spoke. The girls were silent, silent, and then suddenly slipped off all their clothes. "I wouldn't have cared if they were speaking Chinese," he said. "I really didn't care at all. Just as long as it was not Chechen, I suppose."

Everything came to a rather abrupt end. Andrey's mobile rang. He said, "Hi, Mom!" and then went through to the kitchen and did not reappear for a long time. When I went through to make sure he was all right I found him sobbing. A string of saliva ran down to the empty sake saucepan. He'd had a call from Russia to say his best friend had been killed in the war. I felt sorry for Christine. Why had she got herself mixed up in all this? I suggested he should take her home immediately and go out with her somewhere, but he just shook his head, not listening, not responding. Sighing, I called her to the kitchen. Christine couldn't believe her eyes. She had no idea what was going on. "The war? What war?" What war could there be, in a city where for the past sixty years people have only died of old age? Where the most important thing that could happen was that the price of gasoline might rise or fall a couple of cents? It was unimaginable. She wanted to comfort him, but didn't know where to start. She had no way of estimating the magnitude of the tragedy. She didn't read books about war and was nervous about approaching a man who was clearly not in control of his own actions. For two or three minutes she judiciously tried to approach him from various directions with words of comfort, like a large wild animal, a tiger perhaps, to hug and soothe him, but then completely gave up and started wailing, down on the floor, clutching at his leg. He pushed her away, but not violently. I was at my wits' end, and went off to the store at the filling station to get some vodka and tranquillizers.

Along the way I worked myself up, becoming increasingly angry with Andrey. Why was he embroiling this innocent girl in a situation which not every mature, wise Russian woman who had seen it all would be capable of coping with, and even then only if she was prepared to sacrifice herself? What need had this German girl of a crash course in the lunacy of Russians? In any case, people like him should have a stamp on their forehead reading, "War Veteran", and be given a wide berth. Perhaps it was not his fault. Perhaps he was a victim too, but why infect other people with a disease if you're a carrier?

When I got back I put the bottle on the table, took out glasses and tried to disengage Christine from Andrey's leg and lift her off the floor, to no effect. Andrey had stopped crying and was now sitting there silent, angry and menacing. Christine was still flopping about on the floor, shaking her head and repeating, "No! No! No!" Andrey turned to me and said in Russian, "Tell her I'm going to the war." At that I burst out, "Oh, that's really great! Listen, if anything happens to her, I'll... I'll..."

Unable to take any more, I ran into the bedroom, shut the door behind me, and collapsed on the bed wailing in despair. They all came to me then in the darkness of my bedroom, all those German girls from my class whom I had hated for many, many years: Jennifer, Elke, Klaudia, and all the others who were so unfair to me, who upset and tormented me, who hurt me and laughed. Ralf appeared, and the old man from the court case with his granddaughter, and teachers and officials from the town hall. From under the bed a thin, pimply girl, too tall for her age and wearing jeans, awarded each of them in turn a shiny star out of a basket dangling from her arm. She kissed them on the cheek and whispered equally shiny words to them. After each kiss she turned her shining eyes on me, looked at me attentively and, disapprovingly shaking her head, said,

"Remember this. Just remember it." Well, how am I ever going to be able to forget now? Tell me that.

Then the door opened and in crept Christine. She came over and fell on the bed beside me, whispering, "He told me to go away." I gently hugged her and we just lay there, listening to the clinking of glass coming from the kitchen and then Andrey singing about some incomprehensible "choppers in the sky." I couldn't kick him out. I had no right to, though perhaps I should have. Toward morning, completely drunk, he went away of his own accord. A couple of minutes before that he came in to apologize and wanted to take Christine but I wouldn't let him. Thank God, she was sound asleep, lying there like a child, snuggled under the cover, and my heart was filled with inexpressible love for the silly cow. He had the wits to go home on foot or by bus, I don't know which. At all events, he left the car under my windows. In the kitchen, under the empty bottle, next to a broken glass, lay a 50-Euro note.

To Mozdok, to Mozdok soon two choppers will be flying,
Taking us far away from the killing and the dying.
So, farewell, Khankala, as a CO hugs his men.
Never more, never more will we be back here again.

Socialist Village, Southern Kazakhstan, April 1944

Dear Wilhelm,

You know, only now when you and I are parted by sands which show no signs of tears or blood, so that however much I cry I will leave no trace on them, and you remember our wheat fields which hid nothing, and if two people had loved each other the wheat itself would lie on its side like it too was exhausted by passion, only now do I understand what it was I did when I said for the first time that I love you. That was after we were married, my dear. Will you forgive me? I will never be able to forgive myself for having said, before that, no more than that I would love only you as was ordained of a wife by God, and rejoiced in that future love not recognizing that love was already burning in my heart like a prayer, and on whatever I touched there remained a trace of my love, as the towels I embroidered before our marriage remain wet with tears. I have only one left now and I dry Irma with it. She gets out bare and all wet on to the stool, raises her arms and I try to dry her well but she laughs and sits down, grabs the towel and wears it on her head. My dear, I am sorry, I am writing and writing and I cannot get to the point. When I told you that first time that I love you, I never tire of thanking the Lord that he did not take you from me before I, fool that I was, did that because I could have left it too late, and that is too dreadful even to think about, but again, forgive me. With that "I love you" I made a promise to you and to God that whatever happened I would endure everything that God might send and would survive to meet you once again. I will not die from starvation or disease or beatings. I will meet you young and strong and beautiful, just as you remember me and even better. I have learned many things. I have learned to cook whatever I am able to get, to fill the stove with anything that burns, to wear anything that gives warmth. I have learned to look those who hate me straight in the eye, and yes, I myself have learned to hate. When you come back to us I will wash you, caress your wounds with my fingers and lips. I and Irma will spread a cloth and seat you at the table and watch you eat. I will lay you in our bed and cling to you as a branch clings to a tree trunk, and you will know that you have come back to your home. Your home is only where I and Irma are waiting for you. I somehow believe it will be Christmas, and we will have a real Christmas tree and sing Grandma's Christmas carols. Our neighbors and friends will come and I will bake something special, and the angels will come down from heaven to sit at our table because we have suffered but not lost ourselves. They have tried to wipe us out, but they have not even made us lose our love. There is much we have been unable to do in our country, in our republic. We had no time to finish the house which is now just a pile of rubble. In our city our language is no longer heard or our songs sung, but for now you have me and your daughter and we will always be here, my love, until you come back. We will wait as long as is needful, and that is as natural as that every day the sun rises in the sky to light God's world. For as long as the sun shines in the sky you have a home and that home is with us. I remember that damnable newspaper in which it was written that we were keeping Nazi spies and should be deported. Our whole people. At the college our teacher, a gray-haired Marxist, wagged her finger in the air and said the announcement was against the Soviet Constitution and so simply impossible and a mistake. That very day the soldiers entered our town in trucks, and I had to run as fast as I could to take Irma from the kindergarten and was so worried that when you came back we would not be there. There would be no one and you would wander the streets alone and be sure to decide that I had stopped loving you. That is what bothered me most, my dear, how would you know how I have longed for you, how I love you if I was not there. They gave us three days to pack, we rendered pork and poured it into three-liter jars, and Russian officers listed our property, all that we left behind, the piano, the lace coverlets, the cupboard my grandfather carved, the clocks which always cuckooed at a quarter to the hour, and no matter how the men tried or called in clockmakers no one could get it to come out at the right time. It just wanted to warn us that we had so little time, too little to take in the blueness of the Volga and the sky, to pray in our Kirche, to work and sing and raise children, and love each other among the ears of wheat before the eyes of God. But time ran out and now the cuckoo clock is warning those other people who have come to live in our homes and are trying to build their happiness on our suffering that their time too will come, and they will be herded into cattle cars and taken away to distant lands as we were. And their old people too and their children will also die in trains as ours died. They brought us to Kazakhstan, so far from our Mutter Wolga and billeted us in people's homes. If anyone had three rooms, people in uniform came and said "You have too many rooms. You are going to have Germans living with you." Those people did not know the Germans in the Soviet Union had had their own republic, their schools and newspapers. They knew only the Germans they were fighting against, and they hated us, or pretended to because it is easy to hate people who are weak if you do not believe that you will be rewarded in heaven in accordance with your doings. Irma and I got a room and did what we had to do, just as a field has to grow wheat or a branch to grow leaves, we waited for you to come back. Only, if the war between Russians and Germans is reflected here in Kazakhstan, if Irma and I have to look in this mirror and even ourselves are taking part in that war, how pitiable and wretched is what is going on out there at the front. What is it for, my dear, what is it for? They did not leave us to live in peace here, they wanted to take Irma away from me and send me to build a canal where a human life has no value at all, because all over

Kazakhstan and Siberia thousands and thousands of people like me are scattered who are just taking up other people's rooms with strangers who hate us for it. They tried to send all these people away to build something in the forests of the taiga which nobody needed because they just wanted somewhere to move away these people living in other people's rooms in other people's homes. I decided this could not be the end of our story, that I could not die on this canal which leads from nowhere to nowhere, and our daughter could not be brought up by strangers who would give her a different name. Even if I survived, I would be old and sick and what would I say to you when you asked me where our daughter was. So I walked into the office of the Russian officer and did not ask him for anything but just looked him in the eye and said if I could not go back to the Volga, then I would just stay here together with my daughter and live here, fall asleep in the same bed as her and tell her stories in her own language. He had me right there in the office while people were waiting in a line outside the door, and I bit my lip until it bled because I did not want any pleasure from what he was doing to me. After that, Irma and I were able to stay in our little room and now the neighbors are afraid of us and have stopped yelling "Fascist" at my back when I go out of the communal kitchen with a plate of food for Irma. I have got a job in the library where I am surrounded by made-up heroes who live in a world that never existed on Earth, because how can you believe in the good if you were taken away from your home in a cattle car? As I almost finished college, I give the Kazakh women lectures about how the Soviet Union is the best country in the world. I am saying in a foreign language things I do not believe myself to people who can hardly understand Russian and I keep thinking how dreadfully stupid it is for me to be tormenting these Kazakh women with their kind cow-like eyes and not just letting them go home, and wonder why we cannot just live separately, each in our own way, Germans with Germans and Kazakhs with Kazakhs. My ideas will seem simple-minded to you, I know that when you come back you will explain everything to me and I will see that all this was needful and I will be able to live with a light heart and run like a young girl through the fields with Irma and with you and will learn to love the Russian language as I love the characters in their books who ask who they ought to kill next in order for happiness to reign on earth. Christmas will come and the candle will burn and I will hear your footsteps, and that is as natural as the fact that water will boil if you put it on the fire, my dear, my love, my only one.

Maria Stein

ANDREY

The disgrace. The fucking disgrace of it. Ten years in Germany. This vacation has gone on a bit too long. It is the feeling a couple might have who are told, in the middle of a noisy party, their lonely child at home has tried to commit suicide.

Late at night I was awakened by the doorbell. I got up with difficulty, not turning on the light, and looked through the peephole. Christine was standing in front of it, dressed in black. It would have been so easy to let her in to conduct a bereavement session with me, but now, dressed for mourning, ready instantly to share my troubles, as if she was capable of understanding anything, her submissiveness and love are unbearable. I know Valya said to her, "What do you expect? They're all like that after being in the Army. He'll get drunk, smash the place up a bit, and then calm down again." And there they all are, holding their breath, waiting for nice guy Andrey to go ape for as long as it takes, smash a few windows, and then everyone will be able to carry on living the way they did before. But that's not going to happen. You can only take so much. I did not open the door to her. Let her think there is no one home. Trying to make as little noise as possible, I went into the kitchen and started drinking greedily from the tap. The world is gradually coming back to what it was in the Army. I feel right now like I'm waiting in an ambush, in a stranger's house, and if anyone tries to open the door, I'll jump him and bite through his throat.

I didn't sleep last night, sitting in complete darkness with the phone turned off and trying to think of anything that would keep me here, that would make my staying here less than futile. My family? My sister has her own family, her husband and kids; my parents had more than enough of me in Russia in the first two years after the Army, when I drank my way through all they had saved up over many long years. They deserve a peaceful old age without constantly waiting for the next time I freak out, without that frightened look in my mother's eyes as she constantly wonders how I'm feeling today. It's better for me to quietly, decently go, and just admit the obvious fact that I'm a maverick. I'll write optimistic letters home. My thanks to Germany for the ten years of childhood it gave me to replace the four I lost, two in the war and the two after it. I have no friends here. My life has been too easy for them to appear. Some guys tagged along for a while but then had had enough and took off, either into family life or into crime. A couple of them ended up in prison. Who does that leave? Christine who is trying so desperately to be a real Russian wife to me? No. It isn't going to work. The woman who symbolized my final liberation from the past would be a constant reminder of my disgrace. I cannot keep lying to her forever. She fell in love with my strength and my youth, but if I stay here all my strength will go. I'll put myself in the grave within a couple of years.

I was still a child when I conscripted into the Army, and came out two years later an old man. It was a bit easier for me than for the rest of them because I did not care a stuff about the indifference we met with from our country when we returned. From the first moment it was clear we'd been conned and sent to be slaughtered. I decided I was fighting not for Russia but for the Germany I had imagined as a child. The first book I read was *The Musicians of Bremen* in an old German edition. In the Army I often thought about it, remembering a country where the animals had to protect themselves from robbers because there were no decent men there. They had all been killed along with Hitler. I felt like I had to stand up and defend the white houses with beams on the outside, the mills and princesses. So I, Andrey Schneider, nicknamed "Bundes", got through the war and kept my health and sanity. Only afterwards, when I got back home, it became clear that that was the end of everything. We got drunk, fought, broke windows, and remembered our buddies who died. We cried and yelled all sorts of stuff but what it all came down to was, "You bastards, give us back our childhood!" What the fuck use was all that crap we'd seen and knew? I gave in to the same urge. My life was finished. I had defended my own Germany and now no longer believed in anything. We changed places. I viewed my parents as naive children. I carried the TV out of the house, sold it and drank the money. I couldn't bear to look at how they were presenting the war on TV and what they were saying about us. Not that any of it concerned me. I fought for a country that could not betray me because it was safe in my childhood, a fairy-tale Germany, but I felt bad for the boys who had given their lives for Russia. I have not watched a single hour of TV since, not even here in Germany. I could not bring myself to do it and don't think I've missed anything.

As soon as my parents saw how I was, they started preparing to move to Germany. Two years later we left. By that time I could already feel something solid beneath my feet. I had reached the low point of my self-destructiveness and was ready to try moving back up. We were, after all, going to the country for which I'd killed people. I thought I deserved a reward, a health resort, a holiday. I was given the lot.

Even in the transit camp, having just arrived, I found myself the leader of a gang of teenagers. There was something of the Army about it but it was all much easier and more fun, and without the fear. Here we all were in a new place, cut adrift from our bearings, and what we had left behind had lost its significance. I started to feel a teenager again and desperately wanted to catch up on all the life we had fucked up when we were fighting: dates, discos, parties. I was twenty-two and they invited me to go back to school. I agreed and six months later looked eighteen again. I learned German playing football in the evenings. I found it easy, and in any case still remembered a lot from childhood. I'd paid for all this. I really felt that. Every door was open. Where others hesitated, I plunged in and took what was offered. I got a job and after two months bought my first car. A few months after that I took a bunch of guys to Ibiza to party. I even got paid for playing football. It turned out I had talent. Then I decided I'd partied enough and it was time to take Germany's final gift, a beautiful German girl who was born here. I would marry her and live happily ever after just like my parents. I would buy a house. Mom and Dad did not know which god to give thanks to for the change that came over me. And ten years passed.

I started to tire of it all about four years ago. Too much was just repeating. The less keen I was, the easier it was to pull girls. I had traveled to every corner of Europe and now had to fly to Cuba or the Dominican Republic. The problems with my parents started up again. Now they were blaming me for being irresponsible. They said it was time to grow up. I could not see what they were on about. What was there to grow up for? I was already grown up. Lose your marbles, grow old and die? There is nothing interesting about adult life. Anyone who doubts that should take a rifle and kill somebody. Hey!

Then came Christine. Well, I thought, time now for the last part of the contract. A fresh young girl, suitable for a family, not a leggy model, but cheerful, little, brown-eyed. Nice name. She fell in love with me, and even began learning Russian. We went to visit someone for dinner, sat there, ate sushi, and then the phone rang. "It's me, Vano. While you've spent ten years pretending you're still a boy, fucked hundreds of women and sunbathed on the beaches of twenty seas, I was fighting. We took Grozny, lost it again, the same as always, only then I got fucking killed because you weren't there to cover my back. That's all. So long." What a fucking disgrace. I saw myself from outside, and right there in the kitchen where my mother quietly told me over the phone he was dead, drank half a saucepan of stinking warm sake. I howled. Everything came back, everything came back. In ten years I'd gone full circle and ended up at the place I took off from. Your leave is over, soldier. Get back to the war. That donkey, the dog, the cat and the rooster repaid you with interest, not in money, or white sands, or leggy lovelies but in wasted years.

There were quite a few guys who, by the time they met the bullet with their name on it, were closer to me than Vano. Kostya, for instance, the only person to whom I confessed what I was fighting for, who supported me, and together with him we fought for my Germany. Out on patrol he set off a landmine, started yelling, a Chechen homed in and cut his throat. Timur, shot by a female sniper. They caught her and what happened after that I would like to forget, but can't. Or Vlad, the artist. He made it back from the war, became a drug addict, and a year later ODed. In '97. I was still in Russia, went to his funeral in Yekaterinburg, thought I'd be next. Like fuck I was. A year and a half later I was skipping about as good as new, scoring goals. At that time, though, we were all in the same boat. We all knew it was only chance he was dead and we were still alive.

We didn't really think about them all that much. When you were drunk, when you were shooting up yourself, and in your dreams. That's when they came. Or something funny happened, or touching. Or like now. How can I get out of it? He was there for ten years, crawling in the mud while I was here having fun. Vano. Nobody sent him off on vacation. I was with him in St Petersburg before we left, in '98. We got smashed in the communal kitchen. He told me then he was going back into the Army, said he could not find himself anywhere else, suggested I come with him. We already had the plane tickets. I thought about it, but not for long. Decided to gamble on Germany and, as it turned out, won big time. Only who could tell no one would be able to cure me completely? Now I have nothing to defend, no one to fight for. All I can do is take revenge. I haven't given them a thought in ten years, but now, just like then, I hate those bastards coming down out of the mountains. The hatred is burning in my heart and lighting up my path. All the lights will be at green, like here in Germany, and in a few weeks' time I'll be knocking them off with my assault rifle. It's the children of the ones we killed have grown up. Well, we have to finish the job. Hold on, Vano, I'm on my way.

I decided to go back through Petersburg. I needed to visit Vano's mother, to learn the details about how he died, go to see his grave. On the floor below mine lived a Jewish couple from Petersburg, a wizened man with whiskers and his pink, short-sighted wife. Odd birds. They were still in love with each other, every night drinking a bottle of good French wine together in the kitchen. Love with a touch of routine alcoholism. The next day I went down to see them and ask about the quickest way to get to their hometown. They usually flew via Finland and they reserved me a ticket there and then over the Internet. Two days, Vano. Hold on for two more days. I called my sister, explained briefly what was happening, that I was going to Russia and not coming back, asked her to sort out the apartment for me as I would not be needing it any more. I persuaded her not to tell our parents anything. I would write to them from there. That would be easier. I made over the car to her, went to the bank, cleared my account. It took me a long time to summon up the courage to phone Vano's mother, finally dialed the number and said I was coming to offer support. Now, with the future all settled, I would know what to say to her, and feel I could look her in the eye.

I didn't turn up for work. For a long time I was carrying boxes out to the rubbish dump with stuff my parents were unlikely to find a use for. One time as I came out of the house, I felt someone watching me. Fifty meters away, by the building, I saw my sister. She'd put on more weight. Soon her husband would stop fancying her. She was holding on to the fence, saying nothing as I went up and down in the elevator. Poor woman, she'd had a hard time of it as well in those two wretched years after Chechnya. I brought out the last box, went over, looked at her and gave her a hug. My sister kissed me, made the sign of the cross over me and went off without a word. She just disappeared round the bend in the road. I'm going off to kill again, Sis. Not even your love can stop me.

I went round the shops choosing cooking utensils for Vano's mother, only who would she be cooking for now? That was a dark thought. Do you remember those sprats at the Shatoy checkpoint? They fell into some vodka which had been poured into a pot and floated there, looking like rifle parts in oil. All in one, vodka and the snack to go with it. Just before that Vic got wounded, and then they took his leg off in Khankala. I wanted to buy her a sewing machine but couldn't find one the right size. Christine phoned again. I tried to talk to her but all my German was already leaving me, the articles, the endings. I couldn't understand her. In the end she burst into tears and hung up. My mind was already at least in Mozdok.

I took the bus to the airport, the only passenger who was going to war, which is why it was only me that the winter woods and fields, and the white two-storey houses, like the one which I was not destined to build now, were giving a sendoff. Three years ago, one night at a railway station, I met a tank driver in a Russian military vest. Every night he shot into a crowd in his dreams. I was stylishly dressed, good-looking, in a hurry and did not hear what he was saying, did not drink with him, left him alone there aiming his sights, turning the tank armor round. He shouted at my back, “Grozny! D’you remember? Khankala? D’you remember? Minutka Square? Do you?”

I do. Forgive me, brother. I’ll avenge you too.

On the plane I sat next to two huge Finns. The entire flight they were drinking vodka, squeezing it out of little plastic packs.

Then we were coming in to land. The lakes and pine trees grew larger, the land was covered with peaceful, blameless snow. Not the kind you drag wounded men over, the kind for Santa Claus’s reindeers to trot over. Then the small Finnish airport, three rooms at most. I felt I ought to enjoy my last hours in Europe. I’d never been here. The animal musicians of Bremen had kept Finland for me till last. It was a pity I couldn’t find any feeling that I would fight to protect these pines and pretty wooden houses. I could not lie: I would be fighting only for myself and my buddies. That was the only salvation I could hope for.

The Finns from the plane dispersed to wherever they were going to, and I stood at the entrance to the airport waiting for a pre-arranged minibus which was to take me and a few other people to St Petersburg. A woman with graying hair and enormous wooden earrings came up and asked in Russian whether I was waiting for the bus to St Petersburg. I was. Her bags were guarded by a man with a ponytail who looked like an Indian or a Mexican. We walked towards a grimy bus with Russian registration plates. As the driver was putting my bags in the trunk I saw a tattoo on his hand and asked where he had served. Kola Peninsula. Never heard of it.

The roads went past quiet snowy forests or were hacked through rocky outcrops. A Soviet film was screened on a small TV fixed near the driver’s head. The woman with the earrings said she'd been fascinated by South America since she was a child. She went there and, in a focus of cosmic energy on top of a pyramid in Mexico, met the guy, her Indian. He said nothing the whole way. I imagined what it would be like returning to Russia with Christine, her waiting for me to come back from assignments, afraid to go outside in the settlement where we would be in some military hostel. Queue up to do the laundry, queue up to get washed. Our women would peck her to death, and cosmic energy would be neither here nor there.

We reached the border at midnight. I had heard nothing about Russia for ten years. I didn't watch TV, didn't talk to people. Putin? What's he to me? I'd learned how to be liked by German girls and was quite good at scoring goals. I handed the uniformed girl at the border both my German and Russian passports, let her make her choice.

The air is different in Russia, Vano, and there's more sky, a lot more. You can scoop it in handfuls. Twenty kilometers after the border we stopped to refuel. I got the driver to change fifty euros to rubles and went in to the store. I took two bottles of beer from the fridge and asked the assistant for a bottle-opener. A rumpled-looking geezer behind grabbed my bottles and opened them easily.

"What d'you need a bottle-opener for? Just twist the cap. People pick things up and don't know how to handle them..."

In Germany, nobody would dream of interfering with your beer uninvited. Very soon we'll again be taking turns to fish sprats out of a can. I felt I'd woken up from a dream which had lasted ten years. The forests were replaced by new buildings, and we drove into St Petersburg before it was light.

I needed the city center. Vano's mom shared a communal

apartment with seven other families, I think, on the Moyka embankment. I remembered us sitting in our vests in the kitchen ten years ago, singing songs and waiting for their Azerbaijani neighbor to come home. We were drunk and wanted to beat him up. Everyone in the apartment went very quiet. The residents were afraid to come near the kitchen. Only an eight-year-old girl kept coming in to look at us, although she was immediately pulled away by her pale, cross mother. The girl seemed to see us as heroes. She asked us to beat up a kid in her class. Funny girl.

The bus drove all round the new buildings, dropping off passengers, and then there was a bridge and I recognized the dark, wide Neva. We came to a broad avenue. I barely had time to ask the driver if it was Nevsky Prospekt when we turned off it on to the embankment and, shortly afterwards, stopped. I pulled out my bag and the bus drove off, leaving me looking at an intercom with buttons. I read the instructions and tried to figure out how to work it. Star-zero-zero-eight-enter. The door opened and I went in and up to the second floor. Vano's mother was standing in the doorway. I wanted immediately to ask her forgiveness and apologize. Perhaps it was stupid, but I wanted to tell her immediately I was not there just as a tourist, I'd come because of Vano. We hugged awkwardly and she led me through the seemingly empty apartment to the kitchen. It was obviously being redecorated. Several rooms were wide open and whitewashed. She had got one of them ready for me. I think it was the one the Azerbaijani had lived in. In the middle of an empty room smelling of limewash was a camp bed with a pair of linen squares. She warmed up some pasta and meatballs and left. No tears, no heartfelt conversation. I didn't even have time to pull the presents I had brought out of the bag. What did I expect? It was four in the morning. Perhaps she was so cold because when I emigrated, when I fled Russia, I hadn't come to see them, hadn't written. I would have explained this to her if she'd given me ten minutes.

After eating, I went to the bathroom, then to bed. I looked up at the window, orange in the night, and fell asleep without noticing. Got up around eleven and went to knock on the doors to find Natalia Ilyinichna. The apartment was empty. Only in the kitchen an eighteen-year-old girl was squatting on a chair knocking back yogurt in green packaging. She had three and was just finishing off the second.

I said hello and asked if she knew where Natalia Ilyinichna was. She had gone to work, of course.

"Who are you, then?"

"Andrey. Didn't Natalia Ilyinichna tell you I was coming?"

"Oh, I never talk to her!"

In a covered frying pan on the stove lay yesterday's pasta with a couple of eggs. I took a fork, started eating and asked the girl what was going on. It turned out that the only people still living here were Vano's mother and this girl, Masha. The other residents had gone to live in separate apartments on the outskirts. Some millionaire had turned up and moved them all out. Natalia Ilyinichna refused to move on his terms, holding out for an apartment in the city center with a concierge, near a park and so on. There was stalemate. Natalia Ilyinichna would not leave and the millionaire could not take over the apartment. They tried persuasion, then threats, but nothing worked. Masha came back, keen to live away from her parents while she had the chance. The battle went on for a year and Natalia Ilyinichna won. Any day now she was expecting the keys to the apartment of her dreams. Masha, disgruntled, was preparing to move back to live with her parents.

I suddenly remembered her. She was that little girl who had run in to the kitchen ten years ago when we were drinking and shouting and rending our clothes. She had no memory of it.

"So are you waiting here now to see Vano?"

"Vano has been killed. That's why I'm here."

"Right."

I had no idea what was going on. Natalia Ilyinichna just didn't fit the picture of a grief-stricken mother I had imagined in Germany. She was skillfully pushing through an ingenious real estate deal, waging war on her neighbors, while her son, according to this Masha, hadn't been seen here for years. I went off the idea of falling to my knees to beg forgiveness from her.

"So, how is life treating her?"

"Okay. She stalks around in an evil temper, like a bulldog, clacking her heels."

Vano's mom looked younger than my own mother, and better. I had the address of an Army agency which should be able to help me figure out where and how Vano had died. The neighbors in Germany who got me my plane ticket had found it for me. As my meeting with Natalia Ilyinichna was off, I needed to go there, and invited Masha to come with me if she wasn't busy. She stretched, agreed, and ran off to her room to dress. I washed up for both of us.

A few minutes later we were coming out on to Nevsky Prospekt jammed with people. It was wet and noisy, autumnal rather than wintry. I walked along beside this young girl, feeling an agreeable surge of masculine power. I could control her young body simply by walking faster or slower. She was tall and likeable, with curly brown hair, a snub nose, an engaging smile, dimpled cheeks, – and suddenly I really wanted her to write to me when I was out there in the war. I knew if I stayed here just another couple of days I would achieve that degree of intimacy. It wouldn't deflect me from my goal: I just wanted some letters and photographs, so as not to lose my mind the instant I got there. We went down into the metro, and on the escalator she remembered the booze-up Vano and I had had a decade earlier.

"Only," she said, "back then you seemed old, but now you're young and in really good shape."

"There's nothing to it," I replied. "I just age backwards."

We found the dingy yellow building from the address on our slip of paper. I thought I would let her go on her way, but she decided to wait in the echoing corridor, along which tired-looking officers who worked in the records department periodically passed. I was greeted in the office by a colonel, and had a presentiment that he was about to tell me where I would fight, where I would be sent, and perhaps even the name of the place where, shortly afterwards, I too would be killed.

"Hello. My name is Andrey Schneider and I would like to find out the details of the death of my former comrade-in-arms, Ivan Dmitriyevich Leshko, born 1976. In 1995 and 1996 we fought together in the Chechen War."

"Counter-Terrorist Operation," he corrected me.

"In that operation. He was killed a month or so ago, as far as I know while serving his country in Chechnya. His death started me thinking about where I fit into this world, and I decided to return to military service. I would like, if possible, to continue my service in the unit in which he was killed, and to fight in the new... operation. That's why I need to know the circumstances of his death."

The colonel folded his arms and surveyed me in silence. I blinked first.

"Well, Colonel, do you get a lot of men coming in and asking to fight in the war?"

"No, soldier, no." He asked me to repeat Vano's name and tapped it into his keyboard. "Ivan Dmitriyevich was demobilized from the armed forces in 2001. Wherever he was killed, it appears unlikely that it was in the course of defending the Motherland."

"You mean, he wasn't killed in action in Chechnya?"

"A month ago?" The colonel took a crumpled newspaper (with the crossword completed), leafed through several pages, and passed it over to me, pointing out what he wanted me to see. I read the headline: "Chechen Republic Ready for the Tourist Season". "Understand? You can go there as a tourist! The Russian Army is not conducting military operations there. Perhaps you were wanting to fight in South Ossetia and confused the names? It's easily done."

"Thank you."

"You're welcome. Don't stop looking for your friend, soldier. He may still be alive." The colonel was looking at me as if he thought I was nuts, or a small child.

I came out. If the Army was still as shambolic as it used to be, they weren't to be believed, but that newspaper…

"Masha," I asked. "Is the war over in Chechnya?"

"They say it is. We're fighting Georgia nowadays, and then the Americans will be next." She imperturbably twisted her boot this way and that. I felt very old again. The Georgians? I had no reason to hate Georgians. The mention of them didn't rouse me in the slightest. Should I go and kill Georgians? But what if that wasn't where Vano died? I was bemused. What I'd seen as a man's clear duty, to go to war to avenge a friend, was proving less than straightforward. My image of the enemy was melting like the snow on this Nevsky Prospekt of theirs. What was I without an enemy? What else could I focus on in my life? I found out precisely nothing about how Vano had died. Perhaps I was not, after all, fated to take up arms again. What then?

We took the bus back. Masha came with me as far as the Moyka Canal and headed off to college. "I'll just hang out with the girls for a bit." I couldn't get my head round this. What made me think we were still at war with the Chechens? Well, actually, only a couple of years ago there was still shooting, and terrorism, and the Germans were taking Putin to task for what he was getting up to there. Was this really how it had all ended? And what if that was not where Vano died? I looked at the passers-by, wondering which ones were Georgian.

Here I was, back at the intercom. Asterisk whatever. Vano's mum was home.

"Why have you come, Andrey?" She heated me up some more pasta.

"You phoned me yourself."

"I did. When I was going through my son's belongings I found a photo with your address and phone number. I called to tell you not to write here any more. He's dead and I'm moving away."

"You told my mother he had been killed in the war."

"No, she misunderstood. I said your friend from the war had been killed. I have no idea how he died."

"So it might not have been in the war?"

"What war, Andrey?"

"The one against the Georgians..." I tailed off.

"Unlikely."

This was becoming farcical. I felt a complete idiot and

just wanted to crawl into bed, or be back in Germany where my life was still transparently full of meaning. Christine had been in floods of tears as she saw me off to the war. My sister had prayed for me. My parents had built a house and grew things in their garden. There were Russians and there were Germans, and I, a Russian, had captured Christine from the Germans, and then left her because something more important had come up in my life. What was that? A war against Georgians, which Vano had not even been fighting in?

"Andrey, what is more important to you: the fact that Vano is dead, or convincing yourself he died in a war?" The pasta in the pan was getting burned but she seemed not to notice. "Yes," she said, "the war destroyed him, the same way as it destroyed your whole generation. He came back different, sick, but he had no chance to emigrate to a cozy life in the West."

"I've come back to avenge him," I said in whisper.

"Then kill the entire Russian Army!" she shrieked, pulling the pan away from the gas ring and storming out of the room.

God almighty! I trailed after her.

"Natalia Ilyinichna, where is he buried?"

"In Moscow," I heard through the closed door. "In Moscow!"

That would be taking it too far. Was I going to kill everyone in Moscow? Dedicating my future to fighting where my friend had died looked pretty stupid now, although in Germany it had seemed the only honorable thing to do. Had my mother screwed me up big-time: "from the war", "in the war"? Oh, fuck you, Vano, what were you really like? What do I even know about you?

I rushed over to my bag and started looking for the

phone number of Grigoriev, our platoon commander in Chechnya, as it seemed to have been he who persuaded Vano to go back into the Army. Vano told me he lived in St Petersburg. They were almost neighbors. I pulled out my clothing, some T-shirts. It all ended up on the floor. I found my old address book right at the bottom. There was a phone in the corridor. I called. No answer. I went to the kitchen, helped myself to some burnt pasta, ate it with ketchup, washed the plate and called again. No answer. I went back to my room and lay on my bed, staring at the ceiling.

Once in the basement of one of those Soviet five-story blocks in Grozny, we found a little Russian girl about six years old. Special Ops had done a sweep of the house and we could not leave her there. She wouldn't answer any questions about her parents, just wanted to play all the time. She couldn't sit still for an instant, spent twenty-four hours with us before we had an opportunity to send her away from all the shooting. The whole time she played with me and Kostya, hardly sleeping. We fed her all our condensed milk, and she just played and played and played. We were numb with fear, from the shooting, the sight of dead bodies, from vodka and lack of sleep and were in no state to think up games for her to play, but she didn't need that. She was satisfied with us acting walk-on parts. Even without us, worlds were constantly being born in her head, royal palaces and magic gardens with talking animals. When someone tried to pat her blonde hair, she pulled her head away and said something like, "The plinthess is going to the ball, horthey goes clip-clop clip-clop". When she was taken away, the lads, at the risk of setting off booby traps, spent ages looking for toys for her in abandoned apartments. We put them in a box and, when it was full, sent it to her. We heard no more.

I got off the camp bed. It was five o'clock in the

evening and dark. I called again and this time Grigoriev's daughter answered. She said her dad had long since moved to Moscow and gave me his number. Moscow again. God! Once again, no reply. I went back to my room and lay down. Who was I trying to fool? When I had read the headline in that colonel's newspaper I was disappointed, and immediately scared of feeling disappointed. It meant I was upset at not having anyone to kill. Perhaps I have just to cope with the meaninglessness of my life on my own? What if I have no one to avenge? What is Natalia Ilyinichna trying to forget, waging war against her millionaire? What use is her victory going to be to her? Did she even notice her son's death as she was battling to make sure she had a concierge at the entrance? What would I feel anyway if we took Grozny yet again?

And why, as soon as Christine fell in love with me, did I, like a drowning man clutching at a straw, run for cover to my hatred?

I fell asleep and had a dream in which I was shown a globe and asked which people I would like to kill.

I was awakened by Masha looking at me. It was about ten at night and she was sitting on the floor of my room drinking something alcoholic out of a blue can.

"Got any more?" I asked.

"I'll get you one."

I went out to the phone but again there was no reply from Moscow.

After that, Masha and I sat in the empty room, talking. I asked her what she wanted out of life.

"Oh, I want to have lots of children."

"What are they going to do on this Earth?"

"I don't know. Perhaps if they choose to crawl out, it means they don't much like the place where they are now."

Finishing the can, I went to the hallway and called Grigoriev again. This time I heard his hoarse voice.

"Bundes!" he said, "Come on down."

"Look, Masha," I said, going back into the room, "where do trains to Moscow leave from?"

Not far away, it turned out. Go out on to Nevsky and walk in a straight line till you come to a round plaza with a column and a building with lettering on the roof. She told me how to get there but then came to see me off. "Where are you going?" I asked, trying to dissuade her. "How will you get back so late at night?" She just laughed. I left the presents for Natalia Ilyinichna in the kitchen.

The train was leaving in ten minutes and I had to run from the ticket office. I kissed Masha on the cheek, climbed into the car and then up to my top berth. We pulled out of St Petersburg very slowly, as if the city were stuck to the windows and was now slowly being peeled off. Faraway fences, houses and factories gradually disappeared.

In the morning I called Grigoriev from a pay phone at the station. "Stay where you are," he said. "I'll be round with wheels." I stayed where I was, looking around at Moscow. I had been there only once before, passing through on our way to Germany. I would not have recognized Grigoriev in his civilian clothes, tanned and nervous, turning his head like a bird, looking for me. He arrived in a Lexus, on the back seat of which was a bottle of vodka in a box, some salads in plastic packaging, and some cups. "We'll drink to the memory of Vano," he explained. We drove straight to the cemetery. The whole way Grigoriev talked incessantly. I was numb, finally having met up with someone who must know more than anyone else, and not being able to think of a single question. "You got out and that was absolutely the right thing to do," he said immediately.

"We'll drink to Vano, and then I suggest you go to a bathhouse with some girlies but without me. I have a young wife. Then get out, go away again. There's nothing doing here. This country is fucking sick."

"What did Vano do after he left the Army?" was all I could think to ask.

"I don't know! I've no idea! What can a soldier do? He was no businessman, Vano, no politician, no glamour poof. That's why he died."

The cemetery was outside the city boundary, a vast field divided by woodland and, for the most part, covered with black slabs like dominoes. We walked through it almost to the far end, I with the box in my hands, hardly able to keep up with Grigoriev who was striding across the field muttering to himself. He suddenly stopped and turned.

"Do you know how many of our lads are buried here? I didn't know if you were alive or dead. But you're alive. You still look like a boy because you got the hell out of here while you had time. I'm getting out too, to Montenegro in former Yugoslavia. I've bought a house there."

"So how did Vano die then?" With the box in my hands and struggling to keep up with him, I felt decidedly awkward.

Grigoriev shrugged and kept walking. Stopped again. He looked around, opened the gate in the fence of the nearest grave, went in, sat on the bench, and indicated the table to me.

"Put it here."

"But this is not Vano's grave."

"We'll drink first, to all our boys. It's a long way yet." He began hastily getting the bottle out of its box and the food supplies. I turned my head to look at the grave next to which we were going to drink to the boys. The inscription read: "Tatyana Albertovna Shchukina, 1978-2005."

Grigoriev poured the drinks, and for a long time looked at me shrewdly.

"Well, Bundes. Let's drink to the memory of our friends. The ones who didn't survive. You know, the ones who have survived are mostly assholes. I don't mean you. You don't know what's been going on in Russia. I'm an asshole, though, a real asshole."

We drank. It seemed to me that while I'd been in Germany they really had been fighting a war here, only not the one I thought. I did not understand it. I was not in the know, so how could I? Somewhere behind us, a great, noisy city was roaring like the sea, and there the lads who had once fought shoulder to shoulder with me were going into battle. It was a war in which, obviously, people like Vano got killed, and there were victors, among whom Grigoriev clearly belonged. There would be no place in it for me.

By way of apology I downed a glass to Tatyana Albertovna Shchukina too. Then we walked on, Grigoriev going more slowly now, but still with long strides, sometimes clutching at the fencing round the graves.

Vano's cross stood out in the open, with no fence or bench.

"There now," Grigoriev said. "Hello, Vano."

He began to cry. I looked ahead. Beyond some straggly woodland was open ground into which the cemetery would soon be expanding, and beyond that were twenty-story apartment blocks which looked like sailing ships.

"Listen, man" I said, myself staring down now at the fir branches covering the grave mound. "Don't think of me the way I look now. I really have nothing to lose. Somebody murdered him, I can feel that. Why don't you tell me what happened. I still know how to shoot."

Grigoriev gave me the same look that colonel in Petersburg had, as if I were a half-wit. It was a look I'd been getting here quite often.

"Andrey, I hope you at least will not break my heart. Get the fuck out of here back to your Bundesrepublik. Let's give each other a final hug before I get angry with you."

We hugged, half-drunk, at the far end of a vast, cold field in which, under a thin layer of earth, the scraping of bones was probably to be heard. Very close to us lay Vano, alone, far from his Petersburg and the Moyka Canal; far from his mother, her heels clacking as she took possession of her opulent new apartment; far from Chechnya where we were driven back and forth in trucks and armored personnel carriers along muddy roads past people who hated us, who shot at us and ambushed us. And somebody called that a war.

Then Grigoriev brought out the vodka and glasses and filled them. For himself he just wet the bottom of the glass because he would be driving. He put them on the ground while he took out the plastic packages, and I saw through my drunken haze that they contained sushi. We drank the vodka, ate the Japanese rolls, and I worked out to my amazement that barely four days had passed since that evening at Valya's. Grigoriev filled a glass for Vano and poured it on his grave.

"Okay, that's it. Did you hear what I said, Bundes? Quick march back home, soldier."

We returned to the car in silence.

Who gave me my life back and why? Only a couple of days ago I was certain I would die in Chechnya. On the entire planet I now had no enemy, and it was hard to believe

I ever did. Vano had been killed by an unseen force which, I knew for sure, it was senseless to fight against. Yes, I could try. I could spend a lot of time and effort attempting to tease out this tangle, but in the end I would come up against a brick wall. I could feel I'd just be back to where we were in the mid-nineties when we all returned from the war. It all stemmed from the anger and resentment inside us, not from the enemy. I didn't want to start digging in the dirt in which the life of Grigoriev was mired, and evidently also the life of Vano, because I knew I'd been saved me from the same thing by emigrating. Even if Grigoriev had killed Vano, and I didn't rule that out, it wouldn't have made him the unambiguous enemy I'd counted on fighting when I was still in Germany.

There was no more to do in Moscow. Grigoriev drove me to the station.

"That's it, Andrey. Give this to Vano's mother." He shoved an envelope into my hands. "And take yourself off to a sauna and steam yourself with some dollies, and then go home. Nach Haus!"

We gave each other a parting hug and then, without turning round, I walked into the station and bought a ticket for the next train to St Petersburg.

Only then, up there on the top bunk, turning to face the wall, I did what I had been unable do at the cemetery. I cried for myself and for Vano. The anger and hatred which I'd hidden within myself for ten years to protect my life from all the memories of the past, released me, and the reason for that was these past four crazy days. I didn't know what would come my way now, or how far it would provide a satisfactory foundation for my life, but instead of a heavy weight I felt a void and, whatever might come next, that seemed like a step in the right direction.

There followed two insane days in St Petersburg. I was in a hurry to get back home. I needed to reassure my sister and my parents, and try to get my job back. I spent those two days in the company of Masha. The first night we danced at a club. We spent the whole of the next kissing on my camp bed, as though I was fifteen again. In the morning, before I left, I proposed to her.

"Come and have my babies," I said.

"Why, do you love me?"

I replied, "That is a definite possibility."

In the plane I remembered that little girl we rescued from the basement of a half-ruined apartment block and burst out laughing.

From the airport I went straight to see my parents. I found my sister with them and we had a family reunion. When we had a moment, she told me that today she had just plucked up courage to tell them I had gone.

"You bastard, Andrey. How can you behave like that?"

I hugged her. What else could I do?

After dinner I took my father aside and told him I was thinking of building a house.

"Really?" he said, taking me over to the bar. "Got your eye on someone, have you?"

VALERIA

"Are we really going back?" We really are, young Valya. Going back, leaving everything neat and tidy behind us the way Father taught. We have wiped away all the anger and hatred from the city streets. We have cleaned the glass that separates us from the sky and now everything up there is shining so brightly you can't look up. We are taking back with us all the things we once brought: the books we bought with money from selling sweaters, our language, the recipes for much-loved, over-the-top cakes with too much fat for the climate here. Are we leaving love? No. I'll find deposits of it in Russia and send it here along a gas pipeline, and in the market they set up in the central square at the weekends a shiver will run through the hard winter vegetables, and the ladies in expensive coats (here only rich people go to the theater and the market; poor people buy everything in supermarkets) will weep and at long last stop being so stuck-up. After all, my ancestors sailed two hundred years ago to Russia in search of love and only now have I realized they grew it in their fields, they squeezed it out of their cow's milk and sweet corn.

What will we leave behind in Germany? We will leave them the Rhine, given back in the winter to barges and birds. It is weird to think of that huge volume of water flowing swiftly so very close by, absorbing all our greed and folly and sweeping them out to sea where the wind will disperse them and the dolphins laugh at us. We will leave behind us Christine, whose love was awakened by the dark shadow of someone else's war, a girl who made me forgive everyone and everything, or rather, recognize that there was nothing to forgive; the most humane society will always be the most crass, and where death and brutality rampage, the greatest love, pale and weak, will reach up out of the ground to the watery light of the sun. We, the Snow Germans, are now and forever caught in the middle. In Germany we are the people tapping on the glass of the aquarium to wake up the dozy fish, and in Russia we look down on our neighbors for not keeping their part of the courtyard tidy.

Christine has vanished. The day after our ill-fated sushi evening, I woke up because of a flicker of light in the room. It was the neighbors upstairs shaking out their duvets. It was as if a train were going past the window. I made breakfast but Christine couldn't eat. She just sat there in my armchair, clasping her knees and staring into space. She promised dully not to go to Andrey, not to phone him, to forget him, to put him out of her head. I told her that for as long as I was still here, my door was open for her, and I would be glad to chill out with her at a disco. She went out the door and I heard no more of her before I left.

I really did have a lot to tie up. I needed to think everything through, resolve issues with contracts and insurance policies, and spend some time with my parents too. There was no telling when I would be able to come back to see them. On my last evening I gathered up the notes I've been writing these last few months, tied them with a ribbon and left them by the Gutenberg monument. I wanted to make a conciliatory gesture, not to leave the reproachful eyes of the city with the frozen image of me naked in that window frame.

The next day, Moscow greeted me with unbelievable traffic jams, a grimy sky, and a growing sense of jubilation. I stayed the night in a hotel with a view of the TV tower. I had an appointment at eleven at the gas corporation's head office, and stood in the subway car, observing morose people hastening to work, where they would no less morosely look forward to the end of their working day, extract love for the whole world, play office politics, be unfaithful to each other in empty workplaces at night and behind locked office doors, and yet still do their jobs so as to have clear-eyed babies and women crying as they see their men off to war.

I got out in a district of new buildings, emerging on to a broad, crowded avenue, and spent five minutes circling round a patch of ground between a pancake stall and a book kiosk, asking hurrying, serious-faced women who, when I stopped them, became solicitous and flummoxed as to which way to go. Someone finally managed to give me directions. On another busy street I needed to turn left, and there I could already feel something elusive and beautiful, in this unlovely district where, on the one hand identical apartment blocks tended to infinity, while on the other one hideous commercial outlet followed another, and you felt not the least urge to go into any of them.

Then I saw it. In the middle of a vast fenced-off area stood a skyscraper, two towering concrete walls, great stone slabs, and sandwiched between them, there could be no doubting it, upwards, like a fountain, past an unbroken succession of windows, pulsed a blue stream of love, breaking free of the jaws of the vice crushing it, up into the sky – a tower, a jet of flame piercing the heart of the heavens – and doubtless explaining all the grimy wadding in the sky. As I crossed the street, I thought the architect must have felt the same way I did. It had to be here, in this gray, dismal district, from this building which so resembled a medieval tower, in the capital of a northern country, that there should burst out of the ground this inexhaustible flow of energy, and we Snow Germans must return and take responsibility for it, because we know what life is like over there in the lands it has yet to touch, has yet to illumine with its bounty.

Let me pass! My boots may be muddy, but beneath this coat I am wearing a smart business suit. I am young and beautiful and full of dynamism. I can run six kilometers without wearying. Let me and Valya in. Admit us!

The elevator took me up to the thirty-first floor. A young man with thinning hair was waiting to take me to the office of my business contact and future employer. I waited two or three minutes before he stuck his head out of the door and invited me through. He was still just as huge and just as bearded.

"Val, hello!" he boomed. "Good to see you. Glad you answered the call."

I smiled, went in, took the proffered seat. He sat down too, but then abruptly got up again and placed his hands on the table. He sighed.

"Let's just cut to the chase. You watch TV and read the newspapers. Since early autumn our shares have fallen by a factor of five. Five! And over there with you in the West things are, quite frankly, no better. Undoubtedly this is just a blip, but we can't take you on right now. Right now, we can't do it. Six months ago, no problem. We are not letting go the people we did hire. We are not letting them go. But for the time being you will have to wait."

He went on to talk about economic models, cursed the Americans, but a moment came when I could tell he was getting bored. I said goodbye and left. In the adjacent office a girl in rimless spectacles had joined the young man. As I walked down the corridor, I caught a snatch of their conversation:

"Who was that?"

"Oh, it's just the boss at it again. On his travels he recruits expats or people who've re-emigrated and then we don't know what to do with them."

I found my way to the subway and headed back to the center. Inside the area delineated by the circle line I felt a bit surer of myself and got out at one of the stations. This was my first time in Moscow and I didn't know my way about, so I walked for a while and turned into a quiet, narrow street. On one side were mansions, and on the other pre-revolutionary buildings of five or six floors. Snow started to fall and the trees turned their backs to it. In the summer it must be leafy here. I stopped right in the middle of this little side street in front of a tall, handsome building decorated with stucco scrolls. I felt good, unburdened, and I smiled. This was where I and Valya would live. I would note down the address and we would rent a two-room apartment. It seems inconceivable that there would be no room for us here.

MARK

I returned from Russia happy, a thousand times happier, looking like I'd been in a dog fight, with a swollen face and my body covered in black and yellow bruises, the color of an overripe pear. I returned loving and loved, back from winning a war, or rather from a war which had been canceled because it turned out to be just love. Like a three-year-old moving wooden blocks about on the floor, I had suddenly figured that out in the snowdrift. My fellow passengers on the plane shied away, trying to ignore me. Of course they did. I was a Russian, a powerful, ferocious beast smelling of vodka. The Byzantinists, I couldn't believe it, assigned one of the conference participants to make sure I did not escape or get up to anything else before going to the airport and finally leaving Russia. My chaperone was a well-built young journalist and, as our taxi moved off (we split the fare), he leaned over and confided that he had every sympathy with me and that I'd evidently had a cool time. "And how!" I said, and told him how to find the nightclub the American took me to on that first night. In total I'd spent just over two days in Russia. Will you remember me, Russian city of Voroneshshsh, where I was re-born under a snowdrift?

Then our plane flicked like a star from one frame of my

window on the thirteenth floor to the other. I wonder what being was watching its descent in the empty apartment, and whether it remembered to make a wish. The star left a moist, oily trace on the glass and then disappeared. The Earth caught it in the palm of its hand. From Frankfurt Airport to our city is half an hour by train. We trundled along. To me, already accustomed to racing through the night on the roads of Russia, the considered pace of German rail travel was torture. After the immensely long Opel plant there followed two or three identical little towns, at each of which the stop was timed to a split second. You could hear the metronome ticking.

At last the river was flowing beneath us. You can see this exact part of it from my window. At night this was the blank space between two slices of cake studded with candles, but right now it was just the mirror in which the city sometimes pulls faces out of boredom. It has been standing here for almost two thousand years and probably hates its reflection. Someone invisible knocked at the train door and it opened immediately. I walked along the platform, entertaining my bag by rolling it at different speeds over the shiny and, after Russia I have to add, very clean ground.

The path goes through the bushes, our local jungle which conceals the wire fence round the pool like an overgrown Buddhist temple. Do you remember this path? The Chinese are a Russian's best friend; at least, I was let in to my house by a Chinese woman. She went in ahead and held the door open. We went up in the elevator together. I got out at the thirteenth floor while she went even higher, to her Celestial Empire. I cautiously, fearing to startle your shade, took off my shoes and walked around the apartment. The Red Corner, the Green, the Blue, the Yellow – all were empty. There was no scent of you. How can I explain? I don't detect it with my nose. There was no trace of your pollen, those tiny buzzing particles through which you are manifested to me. There is none of the moisture of your lips and eyes, and that is why the room is dry and I'm thirsty. I sit down on the couch (oh, here's the conference program) and close my eyes. If your messengers are not here, if you have recalled them all, that is a sign that soon you'll be here yourself. Someone is squeezing my heart so hard, the way a dog clamps its jaws on a rubber toy, only this is not a toy. O Lord, don't let me die of happiness.

In the days that followed I washed and cleaned the apartment, which had been neglected during the months of my suffering, bought a bunch of different chemical cleaning products, and bags for the vacuum cleaner. I went online and figured out where I stood with the University. I had irredeemably lost this semester but that was water under the bridge. Now I was in a state to catch up on everything. I sketched out a rough plan of the seminars I would need to take and saw I should be able to finish in a year or a year and a half. I took comfort in the fact that I now had experience of delivering political speeches in the international arena. A panicky e-mail arrived from the boss: rumors had reached him of my expulsion from Russia. Critically examining the yellow bruises under my eyes, I set off for the office. Let's just say, I wasn't fired. Oddly enough he found the tale of my sojourn in Woronesch amusing. I skipped the most piquant situations. "How my employees behave outside the European Union is not my concern," he said when he'd finished laughing. "We can treat conferences paid for by the Russian Ministry of Propaganda as they deserve. But tell me, did you also bang your boot on the rostrum? Ha-ha!" I had three days in which to prepare an article about the occasion, which obliged me to retrieve the conference program from the trash can.

The clocks started ticking, time again acquired real weight. I lay on my candy wrapper duvet and waited for Andrey to bring you to me, submissive, your head bowed, a knowing smirk on your lips. Winter was on the way out. My new skin, replacing the one lost in a Russian snowdrift, was already in place. I found out where the Russian store was in our city. It was vast and almost empty. What it had most of seemed to be assistants. There were perhaps five of them, all female, all congregated in one section, chatting among themselves and paying no attention whatsoever to their few customers. I picked out Russian jars, some strange-looking candy, and beer in a blue can bearing the number “7”. Back home, I opened them. Nearly all contained vegetables in oil, which could only conceivably be eaten along with bread or maybe potatoes. I sliced a loaf of bread and washed everything down with the beer. I lived on this for four days. In two jars I found not vegetables but slimy mushrooms which proved also to be edible if eaten with bread. Having consumed their contents, I carefully washed the jars and arranged them on my kitchen shelves. Round beings smiled down at me from the labels.

The first person to come to see me was Silke. She was very disturbed and said I must act immediately and win you back from that crazy Russian who had gone to Chechnya to kill peaceful civilians.

“Do you know what they get up to there? In rebel villages, where a small nation is fighting for its independence – what could be more sacred? – they murder everyone, including women and children, so that there’s no one left to take revenge. You are a political scientist, you must know. And that butcher is missing the sight of blood and so he has gone back there."

I asked how I could win you back from him if he had already left.

"That's the whole point! While he's away is the perfect moment. Oh, Christine is so suggestible. She lacks true democratic feeling, otherwise she would stay away from that murderer. That's what our tolerance has brought us to. We let anyone in to our country who asks." Silke began pacing up and down, transporting her large body from the couch to the bookcase and back. "Really, what sort of a German is he if after ten years of living in Germany he has learned nothing? They had only to whistle and he ran to do the bidding of the latest dictator. It's terrible. They're all the same there."

"Is there still a war going on there?" I asked. Sitting on the sofa, I was getting excited as I watched her peregrinations.

Silke stopped in the middle of the room and looked at me as if I were an idiot.

"The war will continue until the Caucasian republics become independent democratic states. Were Ukraine and Georgia able to do it? Byelorussia was next. Chechnya is next."

"Well, what does Nina think about all that?"

"What does she think?" Silke resumed her marching, with me taking the salute. "Nina is a normal human being. Not everyone who was born Russian, you know, is fixated on violence. Academician Sakharov, for example. It was Nina, incidentally, who gave me your address. She wanted to come with me, but at the last moment something cropped up."

Thank you, Nina. You've got a big heart. Forgive me if you can.

"Wait a minute, Silke. This is very important." Stop the military march. Shh! Fanfares. Lord, give me silence. "Was it Christine sent you to me to build bridges? Did she hint at anything like that or was it your own idea?"

"The fact is that for the time being I'm completely out of touch with Christine. She met some Russian waitress, who was supposedly helping her in her relationship with Andrey. She spent all her time with her. Now this waitress has gone to Russia. To work for that gas company, whatever it's called. A waitress, can you imagine? It wouldn't surprise me in the slightest if she and Andrey have been lovers for a long time. Perhaps they were even plotting some evil against Christine, to recruit her for Chechnya, for instance. At all events, while all these Russians are out of the way we need to intervene. If you still love her, don't just sit there. This is your chance! Nina and I will do everything in our power to assist you."

Then Silke left. She put on her coat, with my Russian jars targeted on her (my kitchen serves also as the hallway). She disappeared downwards in the elevator, walked off somewhere beneath me, then even deeper, and rolled like a ball all the way to the station, as if she had parachuted out of my window. I took my mobile phone, sat down to meditate on the digits of your phone number, then gave it a gentle shake and they drained away inside, replaced by a round dial on a background of your elongated face. It's too soon. More work is needed. You too have been covered by a snowdrift beneath which Russian elves are slowly but surely remaking you, tapping away with their little crystal hammers. How amusing that Silke, in her eagerness to get you away from Russians, wanted to bring you to me in my Russian apartment where henceforth warm fluffy snow will fall every day and, like the flame from gas fields far away in the tundra, there will burn, illuminating its silent falling, the flame of love from my heart. In the mornings, because I am again sleeping at night, a polar sun rises on me and immediately the birds begin to sing to me (in Russian), and by the time I have reached the wardrobe to get some clothes, I have forgotten why I came back here from the great expanses that were opening before me. The world outside my window has become wet and alive, and I can feel it heaving ever more unmistakably, as if the bear is waking up on whose skin we inadvertently built our city. Now it is quivering and people in the streets seem to be in love and out of their minds.

One time I became an insignificant, almost imperceptible dwarf, and I swung back and forth on the door handle because I did not know what to do or where to run to. The Russian jars in the kitchen gathered in a circle and began to dance, raising their legs the way Russian soldiers did in front of Hitler's bunker in a film I saw. I took myself to the shower and, just in case, hid beneath a stream of snow. You sent a text message to say you were coming to see me. Then somebody rang from downstairs, I pressed the buzzer to open the entrance door, and started making the elevator come up, putting all my strength into pulling it by the cable. I was tired. I almost died from the effort. Finally you reached the requisite elevation, the doors opened and you all came out, Andrey, a girl I didn't know (the Russian waitress), and you. They were on both sides of you, holding your hands. You walked silently and submissively and, yes, with a knowing smirk on your lips. Then they stopped and you walked on alone, and I closed the door behind us, and that's all. With a click the world shuts down, like the TV.

"The Voronezh Fleet"
(an article in the *Allgemeine Rheinzeitung*)

A few centuries ago, events in Russia aroused no interest in Europe. Protestants fought Catholics, kings vied with each other to divide the spoils of the Americas, and in the meantime, contrary to the will of monarchs, democratic institutions developed, and free journalism took its first tentative steps. Wherever it was towards which Europe's hacks were directing their attention, it was not faraway Muscovy. All that changed, however, when the Russian Tsar Peter the Great came to the provincial city of Voronezh to build ships. The navy sailing from the city's harbors was to be large enough to cause the newspapers of Europe to report the appearance of a great new maritime power. Hundreds of ships putting to sea one after the other from the river Don were to introduce Russia to the world. It never happened. The tsar's ardor for his grand design in the south cooled rapidly as he was distracted by a new toy, St Petersburg. The fleet for which so many forests in the province of Voronezh had been felled rotted peacefully in its port. The tsar, however, achieved his goal of being talked about in all the capitals of Europe with his later war against the Swedes. A new fleet was built, but in the north. Somehow, though, throughout my stay in Voronezh, I couldn't help remembering the ships which once stood here. Proud masts, sails flapping in the wind.

I was in Voronezh at the invitation of the Russian state, or rather, of its younger brother, the gas corporation, which organized a Russo-German Forum of Young Journalists. Nobody in this city seemed able to tell us where Russia ends and the gas colossus begins, and many of our Russian colleagues indeed saw no need for such hair-splitting. It remains unclear to me who exactly is leading the expansion into Europe, whose tentacles are extending over an area reaching from Tallinn to Lisbon, the barons of the gas industry, recruited from the former KGB, or a state which seems to equate the revival of its former greatness with anti-Western rhetoric. Analysts speak of an "invasion" of the economic system of the Western world and warn that "excessive dependence" on Russia could prove fatal.

So far, the invasion has been proceeding both figuratively and literally underground, through the pipelines that pass beneath our homes, through fly-by-night companies and offshore zones, through the efforts of a former chancellor of West Germany and former Stasi officials who now staff the offices of the gas colossus in Germany. Now, however, a campaign is being conducted for the minds of Europeans. On the first day of the conference the major reproach from the Russian side to western journalism was of bias in its news coverage of Russia. Russian and German television reports evaluate the same events very differently. This may be explicable by the difference between independent media and media fed by the state, that is to say, the gas barons, or rather... Forgive me, I'm becoming confused.

When these reproaches were first made at the conference, I distinctly heard the creaking of masts and the sound of wind blowing in heavy canvas sails. A new fleet is being built in Voronezh, to capture the columns of European newspapers.

Whether it was Peter the Great or Gorbachev who opened Voronezh to the world, it genuinely has unnoticeably become a part of global society. The boutiques of Western companies, McDonald's... on the streets you not infrequently encounter dark-skinned young people, and even Americans. Have those ships that rotted perhaps nevertheless served their purpose? Russia today is no longer on the world's sidelines, but is a country attracting people, if not from Europe, then at least from the developing countries of Africa and Asia. That is all true, but Voronezh is also one of the worst places in Russia for racially motivated murders. In recent years, more than seventy people who had found a new home in Russia, who had came to fill a shortage of manpower in industry, have had their lives ended in this ridiculous manner. We had it explained to us at the conference that there was no need to write about facts such as these, but I shall attempt to do so while the Voronezh fleet has yet to set sail.

Of course, every world power today needs to have... No, Tsar Peter, not a navy; times have changed. A world power needs to have the atom bomb, a pipeline, and natural resources that can profitably be sold on world markets. In the minds of Russia's rulers, the ability to cut off the oxygen supply to others is the main attribute of a twenty-first century world power. The fact that this might turn German apartments into freezers is beside the point. Besides these useful economic attributes, a world power needs the world to love it, and that is why a gas company spends good money on inviting young journalists to Russia. Appropriately, it invites them to Voronezh where a fleet once stood, ready to go out and conquer the world, and where today people are being murdered for believing unduly literally in Russia's new openness.

"The European media too often pursue a policy of double standards, depicting events occurring in Russia in a negative light. Young journalists should seek to rise above these stereotypes. They should seek to give a truly independent assessment of the phenomena of Russian life and concern themselves with consolidating mutual cooperation." Or we'll cut off your gas!

All the Russian media have to share with their Western colleagues is their experience of how to survive in a totalitarian society. The hope is still alive that we won't be needing it. I repeat, while the Voronezh fleet has yet to set sail on its campaign of conquest.

I understand the motives which prompted Russian officials to convene this conference. I understand what results the Russians are hoping for from it. And I cannot shake off the feeling that we are confronted by a fairly conventional attempt at entrapment; the pipeline to Europe is, of course, called "Friendship". It is a moot point whether Russia understands the difference between the mutual treaties binding Germany and, for example, the Baltic States, and a strategic partnership embarked upon solely because of the impossibility of ignoring our neighbor in the east and of our energy dependence. For the present Russia is in no danger of being loved by the rest of the world, or of being regarded as sacrosanct by the European press. And let us not forget that it was once the truth seeping into the USSR through the selfless efforts of European journalists that undermined the foundations of the Soviet regime and contributed to liberating its peoples. Whose fault is it that the European media have ceased to be allies of the current masters of the Kremlin? No, the Europeans have not changed; it is the climate in Russia that has changed. There are increasing numbers of people there who lack air to breathe, and the European press cannot forget them without betraying its principles.

I left Voronezh, accompanied by the cries of seagulls. A navy is being built, do not doubt it. It is growing in size, the wind is blowing its standards. It is being built on money received in return for the heat entering our homes. Only when we no longer have cause to fear a new invasion, only when the fleet has suffered the fate of its predecessor and is rotting in its port, when people are no longer murdered in Voronezh because of the color of their skin, will it be time to convene a conference on peace and cooperation. When that day comes, you'll hear nothing from me but expressions of admiration and my pen will be entirely at the disposal of that new Russia.

"We Need a Different Russia" is the device of the Russian opposition. We heard the same words in Voronezh from officials and representatives of the gas industry. They wanted to see "a different Russia", pure and bright, depicted in the European press, and we young journalists were the people they wanted to construct that idealized image. I can see why they're unhappy with their own reflection, but I vow that we will continue with all our strength to hold up a mirror to these people, at least until the Voronezh fleet ties up at our shores.

Mark Radke, Voronezh, Russia

And may the blue flame of love on the logo of Gazprom burn ever brighter!

THE CATERPILLAR

a fantasy

Opening the door, which was barred with a digital lock, Misha found himself in a dark tunnel with dank walls which even drunks avoided touching. Fetid black air flooded in from a partly open, rusty side door through which, as the boy could feel with his skin, somebody had been watching him all this time. He needed to hare down the tunnel and then for a while it would be easier. A narrow inner courtyard would open up, rounded like a fingerprint of God.

Pigeons would be cooing there, somewhere high above two hundred grams of gray sky would be suspended, and dim, unwashed communal kitchen windows looked out. At least it was slightly less scary there.

Another, creaking, wooden door led out to the entrance hall and the elevator, the dear, comforting elevator which, who knows how, had been cut into the fabric of the pre-revolutionary building. It was coming, like a lumbering hippopotamus, with metallic rattling, and buzzing like a small factory. Right now Misha loves anything that makes a noise. The clattering of the elevator causes the silence behind his back to curl up like a cat. It is a bit scary standing with his back to the staircase leading upstairs, but you only need to turn round for the fear to go away. The gray steps are empty, and the ghostly pigeons peering in at the windows are only pigeons. At one time you had to fear the basement, but that has long been flooded with warm dirty water, above which damp gnats circle but take no interest in human skin. Every night the house, and Misha with it, sails away over this waste water.

His mother rides in this elevator when she comes home. She walks along the embankment, turns into the courtyard and, crash-bang, is immediately in the elevator. (He cannot imagine his mother walking on her own through that scary tunnel.) Sometimes Misha is already in bed and the elevators behind the wall (he can hear them clearly), buzz like bees, but miss their target. One travels on too far, another not far enough, until finally the humming stops at his fifth floor. Twenty agonizing seconds. Perhaps it's only the neighbors coming home, but no, the heels come clacking to his own door, the light is turned on in the hallway, and his mother stands in the doorway, her coat unbuttoned and looking like a naval cadet in a cape.

At the top, like a baby's pacifier, like an orange pimple, a light sticks out. The button has been pressed into the wall and will pop out only at the fifth floor. It's not scary in the elevator even on your own. Stepping out of the cabin, Misha stabs his door with a long sharp key which does not need to be turned. It staggers back, bleeding, and gives way, and then you have to give way yourself as the neighbor advances towards the kitchen in her red housecoat with the tigers. That leaves one final, sixth, door on the way to the triangular paradise he shares with his mother, with the breeze from the sea, where there is light and life, and the bell-like clanging of the trams on the bridge. The key slips round to the right and Misha is home.

In the room the boy encounters the city, the youthful river, the bridge extending, delicately diagonal, over it, seagulls, and behind the buildings on the far side of the river the blue dome of the cathedral. Their room is irregularly shaped, widening toward the window, and has helped itself to plenty of moist freshness through the open ventilation window. Misha has lived almost the whole of his life in this slice of cake with its yellow lightbulb instead of a rosebud, this Bermuda Triangle open to every wind, so that within his own memory the space has had time to shrink and fade a little. The boy turns on the television and starts pressing buttons, and the wind from the bay blows away his fear. When their neighbor has fed her tigers, he will be able to go out to the refrigerator himself.

When his mother comes home and smoothes out the air and the outlines of the room, drinks a glass of tea, opens out her sofa and comes back from the bathroom, he and she will not put out the table lamp but wait for the call. The rattling of the old telephone in the room, whose triangular shape already seems to make it stand on one leg, causes a slight airquake. After that he can just fall asleep to the sound of his mother's laughter and a language he does not understand. At all. It's not even worth trying, and anyway it‘s not interesting, just as long as his mother keeps laughing.

Misha's mother teaches German at a different, far-away school, and once in his skills class he spent several months whittling a heavy, crooked pointer, every day more and more hating the wretched implement and the taste of sawdust on his lips. At his school Misha is learning English, and German is just one of those very familiar things in his life whose inner workings are completely unclear. German is a bit like the refrigerator. One day the door opened and there was Sven.

When the phone calls, which at first were infrequent and fairly random, turned into a nightly ritual; when Misha learned that a man called Sven lived in Germany and for some reason was taking an interest in his existence; when the city, shaking itself and sending spray in all directions, began to emerge from its icy crust, his mother asked her son whether he would mind if, purely theoretically, she were to get married. Both of them felt awkward, water was trickling from the roof on to Misha's hood, and he said he would have no objection.

That this question was unnecessary was all the more obvious for being asked of him, good Misha who never made their life more difficult than it had to be (for which he had often been praised), who slept uncomplainingly on boxes after he outgrew his cot, there being no money to buy a bed. The boy knew (but did not feel) that they were poor and lived in bad, unsanitary conditions, that they had long been at war with the neighbors, that his mother was unhappy, and that their triangular haven was insecure, wholly vulnerable to news from the outside world. Misha could not wish for no change, or for everything to stay the same. His identity had shrunk around the time his father left, and he had no computer or cool mobile phone to stand in for a personality, at least among his peers. Sven had sent money and an invitation. His mother bought tickets to Germany for the end of May.

Sometimes she would take out a textbook of German and sit Misha on the sofa. He had to read dancing words, which were enlivened by the touch of her finger. The boy coped, memorizing how to pronounce the combinations of letters but understanding not a word of what he was reading. After ten minutes his mother would let him off and he would go and read a Russian book, sitting cross-legged on a table which offered the best view of passing seagulls.

The walls trembled slightly from the trams hammering across the bridge, from the sobs of the brackish water in the basement, from the writhing of the worms in their building, half-rotted away like an overripe apple at its tunnel-like entrance. His mother went off and came back with a pineapple, a visa, a jar of caviar, a pair of shorts, and tickets to a symphony concert. In that last month things began to appear in their triangular world from some other, unknown world. Their neighbor replaced her red tigers with blue fish, and the following day they flew out.

In the arrival hall of Frankfurt Airport, Misha stood with an embarrassed smile next to his mother and a tall, thin, balding man in spectacles. The boy had his hand on a silvery luggage cart, showing interest in this miracle of technology which looked almost like a rational being. His mother had said not a word to him about how he should behave with Sven, but from her concerned looks on the plane he guessed she was worried about the impression he would make on her fiance. Accordingly, all knotted up inside, the boy was currently acting the part of an underage cretin, unable to understand the nature of what was happening and interested only in this toy on wheels. That probably made it easier for everyone.

Misha insisted that he should wheel the bags to the car all on his own, thereby demonstrating to Sven his self-sufficiency, subservience, and willingness to communicate. The German talked a lot, joked about Misha's attachment to the cart, and asked his mother something. Even without knowing the language it was clear that in her agitation she was lost for words. The bags soon disappeared into the car and he had to part with his supportive cart. Entering into his role, Misha admired Sven's car with a look full of intelligent interest, and even ran his hand over its smooth surface. A brief dialogue then ensued between him and the German: "Like the car?" "Yes." His mother, stammering, translated.

One part of Misha was observing what was flowing past the car windows. How cleanly and tidily everything was laid out (he would have replied to a question Sven did not ask). Smooth areas of color succeeded each other without holes or tears, the yellow of omelette-like fields, the walls of houses and factory buildings. Inside the all-admiring clown, the non-fictional boy sat like a dolt hewn from stone. Sven turned to the right and, after five minutes, turned right again. The car drove in the entrance of a park. Rose bushes bloomed and in their midst there appeared a cafe with pleasant tables. They left the car and went there. Three minutes later Misha was choosing himself an ice cream from the photos in the menu. His mother suggested one that was less expensive, he agreed, and concentrated on his treat, licking both sides of the spoon.

The surroundings were wonderful. The air was heavy with the scent of flowers, the tennis ball of the sun had just cleared the net of a long, isolated cloud, a lake shimmered beyond the bushes. While his mother talked about how much she and her son liked it here, how pure the air was, and how she hadn't seen roses for a hundred years, Misha watched the reflection in his spoon as Sven and his mother, joined by the hand she had placed on the German's wrist, were transformed into a single being which bore some resemblance to a spider. Sven suggested a swim.

The little beach was deserted. Misha in his blue shorts was standing knee-deep in muddy, slightly rippling water. Patting him on the shoulder, Sven strode past into the depths. He was naked. The water gurgled as it swallowed his pale, skinny buttocks. On the bank his mother laughed and shouted something in German. Misha closed his eyes and hid under the water.

Sven worked in finance. His apartment, which extended from one side of the block to the other, allowed light to pass straight through and in the corridor Misha felt like a fly fossilized in a piece of amber. Having decided to marry, the German had recently moved here from a small two-room apartment and had hardly lived in his new home, which was why a third of Misha's room was now occupied by decorating materials. On their first day they went to look at the city which, compared with Russia, seemed to have had the volume of its street noise turned down by a half, with a predominance of mellifluous sibilants. There were no cars in the center, and people walked on cobbled streets. They were occasionally swallowed by a succession of cell-like stores which extended along both sides of the street. Near a tree stood a group of Russian musicians, remarkable for their pallor and unshaved stubble. One of them them was jerking a huge wooden balalaika about, which looked like a dwelling for Red Indian gnomes. Giving the Russian tree a wide berth, they went back home, got in the car and drove to the supermarket, where they filled a cart (which, of course, was pushed by Misha) to the brim. It rubbed its sides against all the plastic packaging.

That first day in Germany a new creature seemed to emerge from the rose bushes by the lake and the ice cream spoon. This was the Svenomom. It spoke an incomprehensible language, and Misha's main obligation, in addition to unquestioning obedience (The German had to be convinced that he was well brought up) was to ensure that it was always pleased with him. One head had always to be joking and the other constantly laughing. The Svenomom was pleased when the boy pretended that he himself was pleased, so he was constantly looking for things to which he could attach his pleasure like a burr: a watch he had been given, a T-shirt, a storefront, a good lunch, a cartoon film, a trip in the car. Soon (Misha realized) the moment would come when he would be expected to be pleased about the very presence of the Svenomom and its gluey touch (if Sven sat next to him and put an arm round his shoulders). In his room at night, just able to make out the mouse-like rustling of the television, Misha prepared for this moment. The German night was second-rate in terms of the brightness of the moon and stars, and extremely quiet. When the television was extinguished, the sound of the far-off autobahn ran down the window panes without getting through into the room.

His mother, the familiar, much-loved naval cadet, when she separated out from the monster, also served the creature. Sometimes she would come over to Misha to envelop him in a hot whisper: "Say 'thank you' to Sven," "Be grateful," "Be polite," and would then disappear back into the bowels of the Svenomom.

The boy would walk along the amber corridor to the kitchen, get himself some chips, and on his way back to his room look in on the Svenomom to utter the mysterious word Kannman. His mother had strictly forbidden him to take anything or turn on the television without permission. Kannman, a word denoting a humble request, was the only German word he learned during his first weeks in Germany. Sometimes Misha would say nothing all day other than a dozen Kannmans. Lying in bed, he felt he was a caterpillar capable only of silently crawling around the apartment in search of food, which he had to cajole out of the Svenomom with this Kannman. With no emotions, no ideas and no pleasures (apart from potato chips, chocolate and ice cream), the Caterpillar was a mute, inane fat creature capable only of eating and defecating.

The Caterpillar crawled out of its room and, with the aid of Kannman, went outside where it found waiting for it the old bike the Svenomom had given it. The red ribbon of the cycle path led it down to wonderful green, empty streets, where the Caterpillar could reach cosmic velocities, to paths in the park, lakes, flowers and thickets of blackberries.

Along the way it stopped at an empty supermarket by the park and, trying not to look around, broke open a carton of ice cream in the frozen food section. Thrusting two icy cones, one almond and the other lemon, into the pockets of its shorts, it walked quickly past the checkout under the suspicious gaze of the shop assistant. The Caterpillar ate the melting ice creams by a pond, leaning over to wash sticky hands in its reflection.

After lunch, the Caterpillar went back home, the Svenomom warmed up some food for it in the microwave, and it crawled back to its room. His mother married quietly. At the ceremony it became evident that Sven had no friends, and his parents declined to leave Hamburg for a Russian prostitute. At a family council it was decided that the Caterpillar would go to school at the end of August, where he would rapidly and painlessly, as all good children should if they do not want to upset their parents, learn German.

Sven's vacation came to an end and Misha's mother,

who had once transferred from Medical College to Foreign Languages, got a nursing job at a distant hospital, and also enrolled in German evening classes. For the Caterpillar, crawling aimlessly around the apartment on rainy days and spending all its time out on its bike when the weather was good, the day never came when the Svenomom demanded the supreme sacrifice of damp, slithery, hypocritical love.

During the absence of his mother, on night shifts or at her German classes, Sven and the Caterpillar crawled around their parts of the apartment, avoiding meeting up in the hallway. That was the time when the German beanpole and the boy caterpillar with the placid smile on his lips, playing in his room with leftover buckets of paint and rolls of wallpaper, might have become friends, but it did't happen. In July, Sven, intrigued by his wife's hyperactivity, hired a detective to monitor her movements around the city, especially in the evenings. He shoved the contract with the detective agency inside an old magazine, which the Caterpillar unearthed the following day. It came to the attention of Misha's mother and a succession of noisy rows followed. Sometimes, returning home late at night, his mother would start her yelling without even looking into her son's room. On two occasions the police were called: once because the neighbors complained, and once in connection with some petty shoplifting. The boy had been caught red-handed. His mother, who in other times would have been mortified, didn't even notice. Nobody asked the Caterpillar to explain himself.

Three weeks after the Caterpillar started school, its teacher wanted to talk to the Svenomom. A trim, athletic blonde with a strict look in her eyes informed its mother (she came alone) through the haloes of her gold-rimmed spectacles that their school had considerable experience in integrating pupils who could not speak German. The Caterpillar, however, was an exceptional case. In three weeks it had failed to utter a single word in German (which was understandable), but also in Russian. The Caterpillar said nothing in the classroom or during the recess, despite the fact that it was sitting at a desk with a boy from a family of Russian Germans. It was aloof and not responding to approaches or the educational process. The meeting concluded with a recommendation to seek the advice of a psychologist.

Night was falling. Outside the street lights were pouring milk over the sidewalk and walls of houses. The blinds in German apartments squealed as they were lowered. Family men chained up bicycles in narrow courtyards under the wing of clean, solidly built apartment blocks. Returning home in the tram, the Caterpillar's mother quietly wept Russian tears, while through the windows Germany floated by, blurred, jerky, and as unreal as childhood memories. When she got home she went immediately to her son's room and found him there, soft, unfamiliar, among heaps of decorators' junk which he had laid out on the floor in some complicated pattern.

The boy said nothing. He clung dutifully to his mother, but for all her tears and gentle whispers she could not get him to say a single word to her. Sven, convinced he was sharing his apartment with a prostitute and a thief, invited his wife to sort out for herself the little psychopath to whom she had given birth. For several weeks already he had been mortally afraid of the Caterpillar, trying not to be left alone in the apartment with him, suspecting he was watching him, looking through keyholes, peeping round corners, listening to his breathing in the depths of his room. He was probably right, because now the Caterpillar was wriggling like a worm in the most rotten corner of the apartment, not living but dispassionately observing someone else's life, like that creature in Russia, in their home on the embankment. Sometimes it seemed to him that it was he sitting there in the tunnel and looking goggle-eyed at children who ran by, wanting to suck the laughter out of them, gross, cowardly, gelatinous, monstrous, crushed by the massive house down to a last plaintive squeak.

Autumn arrived in the guise of a freshness, as if someone had dipped a hand into a bucket of well water. Several times a week Misha attended the clinic of a Russian girl, a psychologist with the fiery name of Kostrowa who spent more time feeling sorry for the boy than trying to extract the invisible stopper from his throat. His mother was getting ready to move, having already found an apartment on the twelfth floor of a block with yellow balconies, which stood on tiptoe in the midst of a quiet residential district which reached only to its knees. Misha ceased going to school, but began jogging in the mornings with the girl psychologist who had quietly fallen in love with the crystal clarity of his eyes and the wisdom of his silence. As she was running past his house, she would call up and, while the boy was coming downstairs, hop up and down on the spot, lifting her heels clownishly. Then the two of them would plot a rather balloon-shaped trajectory in the rusty foliage of the paths in the park before coming back, she to her not very numerous patients, he to the hole he had gnawed in the far corner of the apartment.

The situation with Sven was resolved to everyone's satisfaction. They signed an agreement that he would not file for divorce (since otherwise the mother and son would have had immediately to return to Russia) providing she paid the costs of his finding and bringing over a new wife, this time from Thailand or the Philippines. Each month Misha's mother forwarded Sven two hundred euros from her paycheck. They had quite enough to live on and, more to the point, only another year or two to wait for German citizenship.

Now there were just the two of them living together, as they had in Russia. Sometimes, early in the morning, when the alignment of walls is still ill-defined and the boundaries of a room have barely had time to close in after the waking of its inhabitants, it seemed to Misha that they were still living in a triangle, the tip of an arrow flying over the city. Perhaps they just brought the geometrical shape of their home with them to their new location, like wild bees or mollusks. Only now, when he closed his eyes again, Misha no longer had any sense of darkness or rot, neither at the base of the building nor in himself.

His mother went to work and the boy would turn on the television or ride his bicycle to the library, where his mother registered him with a vague hope which happily was realized. The houses bent over him, bowing their heads, peering at him through a thousand windows, but up above a strip of gray sky was the real road he seemed to be moving along, while the boy down below was only his reflection. From the library he would go to the psychologist, who was writing a scholarly article on Misha's case. As she analyzed the situation more deeply, she began to hate his mother. It was nevertheless not to Frau Kostrowa that the boy spoke for the first time, but at home, and he did so reluctantly. It seemed to him that speaking would move him out of the category of extraordinary, exceptional children into that of ordinary, chatterbox losers, of whom he had seen quite enough in his few weeks at school. He was afraid too that, if he began to speak, he would have to part company with Frau Kostrowa.

Misha, or rather by now, Michael, started talking again in German, of course. This seemed to him entirely natural. Was it not what the grown-ups wanted? He never spoke another word in Russian, although he could read Russian books. Something had gone wrong in his larynx. Some unnoticeable ossicle had fractured and now prevented him from being able to pronounce the Russian "y" and "shch" sounds, to soften consonants or roll the Russian "r". His psychologist, who jumped for joy when Michael's mother phoned, made an entry in her notebook that evening: "Only the disappearance of the grounds for conflict and return to the status quo in the relationship between mother and son made it possible for him again to communicate verbally. The stress and fear which had blocked the speech function had a further consequence: the period of silence became a kind of incubation period during which the organs of speech were restructured to the requirements of the German language." She put down her pencil, before adding (in parenthesis), "His mother got what she wanted, the bitch."

Soon the city was asleep, bearing in its hands the boy and his mother; and Sven, sleeping next to a coffee-coloured candidate, invited from a distant southern land, for the position of wife; the psychologist Frau Kostrowa; and many others who rolled about in its hands like peas. Meanwhile, somewhere in Russia, shaking off the limewash and rot, a caterpillar emerged from a cellar, crawled slowly to a small circular courtyard, and soared off suddenly into the heavens, transformed into an angel.

COMPLETE GLAS BACKLIST

Peter Aleshkovsky, *Skunk: A Life*. Bildungsroman set in today's Northern Russian countryside

Vasil Bykov and Boris Yampolsky, *The Scared Generation*, two novels

Alan Cherchesov, *Requiem for the Living*, a novel. Extraordinary adventures of an Ossetian boy against the background of traditional culture of the Caucasus

Vlas Doroshevich, *What the Emperor Cannot Do*, *Tales and Legends of the Orient.* Highly relevant parables about the eternal conflict between the authorities and the people

Asar Eppel, *The Grassy Street*. Striking stories set in a Moscow suburb in the 1940s

Nina Gabrielyan, *Master of the Grass*, long and short stories by a leading feminist

Maria Galina, *Iramifications*, a novel. Adventures of today's Russian traders in medieval East

Nikolai Klimontovich, *The Road to Rome*. Naughty reminiscences about the later Soviet years

Sigizmund Krzhizhanovsky, *Seven Stories*. A rediscovered writer of genius from the 1920s

Leonid Latynin, *The Lair*, a novel-parable, stories and poems

Mikhail Levitin, *A Jewish God in Paris*, three novellas

by a world-famous stage director

Anatoly Mariengof, *A Novel Without Lies*. The turbulent life of a great poet in 1920s Bohemian Moscow.

Larissa Miller, *Dim and Distant Days*. Childhood in postwar Moscow.

Irina Muravyova, ***The Nomadic Soul***. A family saga about a modern-day Anna Karenina

Alexander Pokrovsky and **Alexander Terekhov,** ***Sea Stories. Army Stories***. Realities of army life.

Portable Platonov, a reader. For the centenary of Russia's greatest 20th century writer

Valery Ronshin, ***Living a Life, Totally Absurd Tales***

Lev Rubinstein, ***Here I Am***. Humorous-philosophical performance poems and essays

Alexander Selin, ***The New Romantic***, satirical stories

Roman Senchin, ***Minus***, a novel. An old Siberian town surviving the perestroika dislocation

Andrei Sergeev, ***Stamp Album***, *A Collection of People, Things, Relationships and Words*

Andrei Sinyavsky, ***Ivan the Fool***, *Russian Folk Belief*, a cultural history

Boris Slutsky**:** ***Things That Happened***, by Gerald Smith. Biography and poetry of a major 20th century poet

Andrei Volos, ***Hurramabad***. A novel in facets. Post-Soviet national strife in Tajikstan.

ANTHOLOGIES

Beyond the Looking-Glas, Russian grotesque revisited

Booker Winners & Others. A selection of mostly provincial writers

Booker Winners & Others-II. Samplings from the Booker winners of the early 1990s.

Bulgakov & Mandelstam. Earlier autobiographical stories

Captives. Victors turn out to be captives on conquered territory

Childhood. The child is father to the man

Jews & Strangers. What it means to be a Jew in Russia

Love and Fear. The two strongest emotions dominating Russian life

Love Russian Style. Russia tries decadence

NINE of Russia's Foremost Women Writers. Collective portrait of women's writing today

Revolution. The 1920s versus the 1980s

Soviet Grotesque. Young people's rebellion against the establishment

Strange Soviet Practices. Stories and documentaries illustrating inimitably Soviet phenomena

War & Peace, army stories versus women's stories: a compelling portrait of post-post-perestroika Russia

A Will & a Way, women's writing of the 1990s

Women's View. Russian woman bloodied but unbowed

THE DEBUT SUBSERIES FOR YOUNG AUTHORS

Squaring the Circle. Collected stories by winners of the Debut Prize

Mendeleev Rock, two short novels about modern-day urban life.

Off the Beaten Track. Stories by Russian Hitchhikers.

Arslan Khasavov, *SENSE*, a novel about today's political struggles.

Still Waters Run Deep. Young women's writing from Russia

Alexander Snegirev, *Petroleum Venus*, psychological tragicomic novel about a lone father of a Down-syndrome boy.

NON-FICTION

Michele A. Berdy, *The Russian Word's Worth*. A humorous and informative guide to the Russian language, culture and translation

Contemporary Russian Fiction: A Short List. Eleven major Russian authors interviewed by Kristina Rotkirch, a Swedish journalist.

Nina Lugovskaya, *The Diary of a Soviet Schoolgirl: 1932-1937*, the diary of a Russian Anne Frank

Alexander Genis, *Red Bread*, essays. Russian and American civilizations compared by one of Russia's foremost essayists

A.J. Perry, *Twelve Stories of Russia: A Novel, I guess*